a + e

a novella

A tRaum Book
Munich, 2021

a + e

by Ryszard Merey

Book I - Spring

–Should I cut your hair?

It's 6:30 a.m. Dripping dark outside.

He glances, but not at her. At his reflection. He doesn't have to look to know that she's reddening. When his head moves, he can see a ghoul follow him symmetrically in the black mirror of the window. Tracing the movement of his living form. He knows the suggestion is a gentle hint. Your hair is getting too long. But he likes how it is right now. Is that wrong? He says:

–I think I'll leave it.

–Are you sure? Just a trim...

–It's fine.

–Okay.

She steps close, puts her arms around him. Sickness rises up in his throat, though he doesn't feel sick. Not really. This is just the feeling his body had taught him to replace something *worse*. He wants to push her away—he wants to not, even more. When her arms tighten around him, he lets himself.

–Are you nervous? -He asks quietly, eyes closed. Impulsively, he puts a kiss on her skull through her hair. His eyes squeeze tighter. As if they were shut and he couldn't see, God couldn't see him either. *I wish I could go somewhere where nobody sees us. Nobody sees me. Not even God.*

She leans her head on his shoulder.

–A little nervous, I guess. But I'll be fine. Right?

–Of course.

–You too?

He's stopped believing it, but he still smiles into her hair.

–Sure.

She turns away. Grabs her coat, and they leave together.

It's a new place.

It's a new school.

It's a new day.

To Gordy

1.

The Short One grabs him by the arm and he flinches. Tall One steps right over. Eye contact.

–So, what are you?

–...

–Come on. Answer me. Are you a guy or are you a girl?

–...

–Are you a faggot?

–Why don't you check? –The Shorter One suggests and the Tall One laughs. Says to him:

–I think you're in the wrong bathroom.

Do not touch me.

One of them shoves him into the first empty stall. Reaches for his waist, swipes another hand across his chest under his flannel, as if to check for something. He pushes back hard which is when Tall belts him across the face. Short grabs him from the side. He feels his arm twist until he sits down on the toilet, almost stunned, balancing himself on the rim. Tall says quietly, 'hold him.'

No no no do not touch me, do not fucking touch me, there's nothing you can do just breathe deep, they're not going to hurt you, just breathe deep, close your eyes and it will be over soon, whatever they want it will be over soon, whatever they want, it will be over soon, it will be over...

–I don't know, dude, –Short says. –He's sweating like crazy and he looks like he's going to puke. Maybe we should stop.

–Hey, I'm not gonna hurt him. You hear that? I'm not going to hurt you, okay? I just want— to have—a look.

Short One screws his arms behind his back tighter; something pops in a way it's not meant to.

Breathe in.

Breathe out.

Breathe in.

Breathe out.

Then his chin is grabbed; face turned up.

Forced to stare.

Five seconds of sweat rivulets down his forehead—

Tall whispers:

–Fucking A, you really are a—

And kisses him on the lips.

Tongue pushes into his mouth and he yells, which is when he is hit in the face, harder this time. A vein in his nose gives, the blood comes down and when he roughly turns his head, droplets fling against the stall's side. Wrenching, leaning over the toilet, the two cry out while he heaves—ugh.

A voice pierces their violence. The heavy bathroom door bangs open, and the two bounce out of the stall.

–What the hell is going on in here?

Mr. Rein is a large, perpetually tired man who has spent a decade cleaning in the public school system. So he has seen every shade of senseless torture. He was just passing by to get to the second floor storage room when he heard the yells. Now he is only mildly surprised to find the bathroom occupied by a mess of bloody boys. These kids are fucking animals. He glances past them towards the stalls.

–Is someone back there?

–Just clean up the blood, grandpa, before someone gets AIDS. –Tall pushes past him, pulling the other behind. Rein watches their Nikes track rust across the floor.

Grandpa, I'm 36. Little pricks.

The door of the stall swings open.

When he looks in, the kid is still balancing on the toilet rim. A single tear traces down his face, cutting a path through the blood and sick. His lips look bee-stung, swollen (from the beating?).

Rein breathes out:

–Lord, what a mess. I'm so sorry, sweetie, are you okay?

Hiccough. No answer.

–Those boys forced you to come in here? Give me their names, I'll report them to the principal. This is disgusting.

The student speaks, and he isn't sure what he was expecting, but—

The voice is resigned. Grim.

Deep.

–I don't know their names. This is my first week at this school. And I came in here myself. I'm supposed to be in this bathroom.

Their eyes meet. Rein thinks:

Fucking A. You really are a—

Aloud, he only says:

–Sorry about that. Son. ...Maybe you could get a haircut? It might make things easier for you here.

1.1

Birds are not awake yet.

He sits on a chair placed over a towel, and she takes a small compact; flashes him the back of his head in the big mirror over the dresser.

–Good? More?

–That's perfect.

It's true; she's done a good job. Better than good. Nor did she say a single word when he came up to her, holding scissors. He thanks her and she snaps the compact shut, puts a few more things in her school bag, while he cleans up the towel and throws away the thick chunks of light brown hair.

–Are you coming? –Hope tinges her voice, but he shakes his head.

–I've got more homework to finish. And you have that dance team thing...

Excuses (he could finish the homework just as well in the empty cafeteria, while she joins other hopefuls for the early orientation) but he can't do it today. He can't walk next to her today and clench his fist in his pocket. He pretends to be irritated, looking for something, and she takes the hint. Mutters a 'see you later' over her shoulder. Guilt prickles through him, but the moment he hears the front door shut downstairs, he breathes easier.

Goes to her dresser. She has makeup on it; foundation and a few palettes from the drug store. He takes a tiny dab of flesh-colored liquid, leans to the mirror. Smears and blends it over his lips. He'd discovered this trick last year. It made your lips look... de-emphasized. Less feminine. He can use her makeup; him and her have the same complexion. They have the same everything, in fact. People still ask if they're twins. But they're not the same, not exactly: He's got thirteen months on her. A good inch of height. Broader shoulders. His hair is two shades darker.

He glances at his silhouette in the mirror, looks away sharply—Downstairs, the door opens again (talking). His parents will smoke a cigarette now; throw a bag on the counter (donuts, sweaty with sugar) then go to bed. The donuts are for him and her, but he won't take one. Not that he couldn't: Lena eats everything, and she is just as tall and lank. He could eat. But he hates the sensation of the mashed up food in his stomach. The stomach becomes a fleshy sack clutching vomit. To be pressed into a substance more disgusting. Gurgles, awful acidic churning. Like painting a picture using only bile and uncooked salmon color. Why was life nothing but a neverending rainbow of nasty sensations, ranging from unpleasant to horrifying?

No, that's not true.

There is good. He knows that there is.

He looks at the makeup again. Maybe tonight, he will offer to do her face. Make up for the harsh parting this morning. He thinks of the first time she had asked him to put on liquid eyeliner for her. She was amazed at how well he did it. His hand was steady as a surgeon's, and he cut her a bladesharp wing. That was back in middle school. After that, he did many looks for her. He didn't know the looks had names; he was just using the few cheap brushes she had and trying different combinations. Seeing what happened when you layered the colors or used foundation and common scotch tape to mask certain areas. Using lipstick as eyeshadow and eyeshadow as blush. Scattering shimmer on matte.

–You're too good at this! It's not fair! –She'd laughed, while he transformed her perfect ten face into a perfect fifteen. And he shrugged. It was easy. The brushes, the colors, the lines. They made sense. He didn't know how, but they just did. Wasn't it like paper? (Start light, you can always go darker. Don't pile, layer. After layer. Be patient. Go slow. Step back. Take it in. See what's messed up. Fix it before you go on. And blend.) And he knew her face more than he knew his own. They didn't have a phone or a camera, so they never recorded the looks. But sometimes, he would draw her portrait when she particularly liked what he'd done. He hadn't drawn her for a while now, making excuses when she asked, but back then, he still would. Then he'd wipe the makeup all off. *There's no way you're going anywhere looking like that.*

She'd blush then, because she liked when he was protective of her. Possessive of her.

And he liked that she liked it—

And he hated that he liked that she liked it.

He gathers his sketchbook now, and his Discman and his earphones. He knows, something has to change. Probably him. He's the problem. The aberration.

The past smiles slyly, the past says: I was better. And maybe it was. Back then he could enjoy things, without asking what it meant. He could fill sketchbook after sketchbook with her face. Knowing how much she loved being drawn by him. He could walk home with her and talk and not think. Riva only spoke English for Sam's sake, and the two of them spoke perfect English by now, but they didn't want to forget. So they would talk in their language when Sam wasn't around. Lena would tell him about her day, grip his hand—an intensity would spread through him, similar to that moment right after you finish a drawing. Warmth and love flooding your cells. (How could certain physical sensations feel so awful? And others, feel so incredibly incredibly good?) Like a supreme peace. Or a blessing. For years and years, that's what she was to him. Lke lines, colors and shadows. A blessing. Until that school. Not the last school they were at—but the school before that—the pack of grade-schoolers rushing to the chain link fence, chanting and chanting:

The worst was the looks the older kids gave them as they passed by. After that, he couldn't pretend that he was being too sensitive, that nobody else noticed; that it was normal. Lena shrugged it off so easily, but he never could. These days, when she embraces him, or brushes his hand and the warmth floods his body, he's reminded. The feeling that he thought was a blessing—it's a curse.

2.

He sits alone at a lunch table. Sitting alone, food untouched in its paper bag. He'd told her so many times: You don't have to make me anything. I'm just going to throw it away, and then she would furrow her brow. You have to eat. I know that. But I won't. You might. If it's there, you might. Maybe today. At first, she would pack him the food she thought he would like: plain bread (no mixing of milk and meat, and no lunch meat or cheese, even separately. If a food was supposed to be cold, he would only eat it cold, right out of the fridge); cut up fruit (no abrasive skins or cores); juice. A straw, with the flexy bend. He appreciated her detail for the aesthetic and texture of the food, but since he still never ate anything, after a while, she just made a duplicate of her own lunches: bread, with the lunch meat put directly on. Bruised, sad pears. If lunches are personalities, Lena's lunches are practical, nourishing and conventional. His are void. Eating only when he absolutely has to. Expelling only when he must.

His notebook is out now, his left hand moves over it, music pulses into his head through big headphones, the world doesn't exist, only the paper and his left hand, smearing carbon in a trance. If you set the song on loop and put the volume just so, the entire lunch period could slip away, slicker than a sleeping pill. He's never been one to think about killing himself, no matter how bad things got, it simply wasn't something that entered his mind— but he was an expert on how to kill time. And if you killed enough of it and enough of it, well eventually, all of this would be ove—

A hand rests on his shoulder, another rips the headphones from his ears and the kid shudders.

–Hey there, beautiful.

Tall sits next to him, puts the headphones down on the table.

–Nice haircut. Some girls look even better with short hair.

Tell him to go away

Tell him to go away

Tell him to

–Fuck. Off.

That works, I guess.

He bites his lip, Tall grins.

–I hope you don't kiss your mom with that mouth.

–No, but I'd kiss yours.

–Let's talk about that after school. Is it a date?

It's not the usual harassment. Even if it's supposed to be a joke. If he dared, he'd ask the Tall Kid: You liked kissing me that much? He turns his head instead.

–Why can't you just leave me alone?

–Why can't you just leave me alone? –He's mocked precisely, for tone, pitch, everything, and he blushes. Tall says, –Because you're breathing. Hey, what you got there?

Tall reaches for his notebook.

–Nothing. –Panic rises in his chest and he clutches the book to himself fiercely. The other laughs and pulls it from him.

–Let's see. Secrets don't make friends...

–Stop it!

–So there's something good in here.

–Give it back!

–Hey there honey, is this creep bothering you?

They both look up, surprised—

The girl (??) standing above them blows a Chernobyl-colored bubble with her gum and pops it loudly. She daintily picks off the piece that sticks to her cheek with two pinced talons. Behind her stiletto nails, a knife-sharp jaw, a mess of eyeliner. Her thick almost tar-black hair is completely shaved on one side of her head, exposing an ear with more piercings than earflesh.

Tall sneers.

–Great, the other freak. Shouldn't you be off skinning a rat or something?

–Never mind what I should be doing. Why you bugging the new kid?

–This little prick got me detention yesterday.

–Yah. I bet you were just minding your own business and he got you in trouble.

–What's it to you?

–And what's it to you if it's something to me? Nothing at all, so do us a good, and fuck out of my visage!

Tall stands up abruptly, teeth clenched; she flashes a smile. Both of them standing, she clears him by a cool inch.

–Yeah that's right, –the girl's cackling. –Keep it moving, bitches.

A lunchroom monitor looks towards them for confirmation of a conflict. Tall waves lamely; the monitor looks away, and he turns back to her. Lowers his tone.

–I don't hit girls, so you're fair game. Catch you out of school one of these days.

–Remind me to get scared. Really.

–You're dead, dyke. –Tall plastic-smiles, turns and leaves and she's still laughing, sinking into the vacuum of his empty space. Next to her, he's leaning forward, slightly rigid, slightly awestruck, scrabbling to put his headphones back over his ears before she can start a conversation. His shaking fingers are a beat too late.

–Mind if I have a sit?

He grimaces.

–It's a free country. Kind of. And you're already sitting.

–You've got a mouth on you, new kid. Maybe I should've just let him wipe the cafeteria floor with you. Where's my thank you?

–...Thanks.

–Too late. Pass me your player?

–What for?

–Cause the very last song on it determines whether or not I kick your ass.

He stares (is there anyone in this school not offended by my existence) and she grins.

–Because I'm curious if you're listening to anything good. Duh.

He shrugs and passes her his headphones. She slips them over her thick mane of hair, and he presses play. After ten seconds, she starts nodding. Some hmm's come out of her throat.

–Hmm. "Scentless Apprentice." All right. All right. So... who's Maynard James Keenan?

–Uh, the lead singer for Tool?

–That's right. And what was the better song on *The Bends*—"Let Down" or "Iron Lung"?

–"Let Down" wasn't—

–On *The Bends*. Yeah, I know. It was a trick question.

Her teeth are white and crooked; her face as translucent and cratered as the moon. She makes to clap him on the shoulder and stops her hand when he visibly flinches.

–Damn, boy, two for flinching! Did you think I was going to hit you?

–N-no...

–Well chill out, then. You're jumpier than a cat on speed.

He picks at the cover of his sketchbook. That strange, sullen tone again.

–W-why ...are you even talking to me?

–Because you dress like good music, I see you drawing in the cafeteria every day, and oh, I don't know... you're fine as fuckkkkkkkkkkkkkkkk.

A theatrical wink and fanning of her face, and he flushes so hard, she starts to laugh.

-Don't pretend like you don't know it. That's SO dull.

He runs a hand through his hair and says nothing; and the girl grins again.

-Stay humble then. Your choice. But it's true. You've got the local boys all riled up. Now they got to figure out if they're gay or bi or whatthefucksexual. And in their screwy little raisin minds, that's somehow your fault. I see that bruise on your face. They did that, didn't they?

He nods and she sticks out her hand, puts it on her hip. Big, pale hands, encased in lace gloves, cut out at the finger tips to expose her claws.

-I'm Eu, by the way. It's short for, -Insert a dramatic sigh. -Eulalie, but my grandmother on my dad's side made them swear they'd pass it on. On her deathbed. There's a whole story behind that, involving a dead horse and a McRib sandwich, remind me to tell you sometime. It's all solid gold. And what's your name?

-Ash.

-Just Ash, or... You're not Asher Machnik?

-...How did you..?

-Because I saw your name on the roster of the drama club when school started and I was like, holy shit, this school finally has another jewfish. Maybe.

-Well, we're not practicing...

-Yeah, my mom is Jewish, and we still go over to my aunt's house for Seder, but that's it. I was in Hebrew school for two minutes once...

He has a vague memory himself, of when they still

went to Rosh Hashanah and Passover with his grandmother, and getting into fights over him not wanting to eat anything they served there. The bell ending their lunch period cuts off the memory.

Eu(lalie) gets up and so does he and only then does he really notice how tall she is. He himself is not particularly short, but the top of his head still only comes to her eyes. The huge trenchcoat covering her swings open; under it she wears some kind of loose tank top; under that, bandages on her torso. Seeing him look makes her pull the coat shut, and he shrugs, walks to the trashcan to drop his full lunch bag into it.

Eu coughs.

–Wait. ...You're throwing your lunch away?

His hand freezes over the trashcan.

–I was going to. I'm not going to eat it.

–A bad lunch?

–No. I don't like ...to eat. ...Lunch.

He looks embarrassed, like he has never considered how strange that sentence sounds out loud. Eu sighs.

–Lucky. I wish I didn't like to eat lunch.

He rummages through the bag.

–You can have some of it, if you want. I've got a chicken sandwich. An apple. A synthetic cake thing.

–I'll take it.

–Which one?

She reaches and takes the whole bag. He stares.

–You can eat all that?

–Does the Pope shit in the woods?

They walk and keep talking—food flies in all directions. He is more fascinated than disgusted, watching her finish the sandwich with alternating bites of snack cake while holding a conversation. She looks up, catches him smiling. A careful, mouthclosed smile, but a still. She says, –Dang boy, you're even cuter when you smile. You're a real heartbreaker, did you know that?

The truth is Ash had yet to break anyone's heart, but oh, if poor Eu only knew!

3.

Dramateacher twirls a pencil in his fingers, then stands up. –Alright, so the next two people to try out for the roles of John and Clarissa: It's going to be. –He looks down at his paper. –Avery Beleibt for Clarissa and Asher Machnik for John. Go on up.

Ash walks up to the stage and meets his classmate Avery in the middle. He reddens when he looks at her, because she had already been studying him, critically, he imagines, but the lights blast the area with heat and he hopes his color will go down as their effect. Looking out over the audience, he can't see a thing. The teacher's voice booms from the back of the small theater.

–I'd like to switch scenes now. I want to see chemistry from the next few groups, because the tension between John and Clarissa is really important for the play to work. Now, the fight scene is an obvious choice, but I actually want you to do Act II, Scene Two. This, you will recall, is the scene where John tries to confess his confused feelings to Clarissa, and she, in the emotional upheaval of the moment, grabs him. So we'll keep it rather short, start on page 20, line 48, where Clarissa says "Want to sit?" and end right after the—

After the
after the
after the
Ash is wondering what he could have possibly done in this life or the last to have pissed off the Creator of the Universe with his Pathetic Existence, surely, his crimes must have been multitudinous and vast if after having signed up for drama class merely because it was the only elective that fit with his schedule, and after telling Dramateacher he was not really so interested in trying out for the year's first show anyway, being a more scenery-painter and backstage type of guy (or did they need a makeup artist?), fate still found him trudging down a tracklit aisle after an Extremely Attractive and Popular Girl he was now supposed to KISS. ASSERTIVELY. In front of thirty odd other people.

Dramateacher hollers:

–And begin!

Ash drops his script right off the bat. His palms feel wet as he bends over to retrieve it and he worries about leaving a sweat–print on the borrowed script. He can't gather if it's real or imagined, but Avery already seems exasperated with him, method acting at its finest. There is absolutely no way he can go through with this without puking, and there is absolutely no way he can puke on a pretty girl, and there is absolutely no way he can stop the scene and not forever cement in everyone's mind that he is an irretrievable reject, so he continues to mumble his lines (he only has about three left) while silently praying.

One line left.

Bile in the bottom of his throat. Thank god he hasn't eaten anything since last night...

Zero lines left.

The script doesn't call for it but he closes his eyes and shudders.

He waits for the block, for Avery to grab him and kiss him and for his life to end.

But a second passes. And another.

He is ungrabbed.

He is unkissed.

He is undead.

Ash opens his eyes—Avery has her hands crossed across her chest, not anywhere near him, as she is supposed to be, and not looking anything like Clarissa should be looking at that moment.

–I can't do this, –she blurts.

Dramateacher is nonplussed. –Is something wrong?

–Yeah, something's wrong! I have to kiss *him!* I mean, no offense but he looks like an *anorexic lesbian.*

No offense taken.

Thanks, God.

Also, please kill me?

Amused disorder crawls out of the dark.

Dramateacher raises his voice to quash it:

–Avery, you are not kissing Mr. Machnik. I don't *care* what your feelings are for Mr. Machnik. You are kissing John—John, who you have grown up with, who you have loved since you were a child and who now, you believe, you may love romantically. That is who you are kissing.

–I can't though. Can I read with someone else?

–Everyone's partner is randomly assigned for this audition. It would not be fair to let you pick someone else.

–Then I guess I won't audition.

She shrugs and walks off stage and Ash stands with his head down, rained in humiliation. Meanwhile, Dramateacher is asking if someone else would volunteer to go up and read with him. They would have to read with him, and then again, with their assigned partner.

–Please, will anyone read Clarissa with Mr. Machnik?

Ash wants to tell him to not bother, but the words stick in his throat. The double-blade of being rejected even as a pity-read hovers over his head, so he starts to walk off stage, when someone calls out.

–I'll read Clarissa. Can I?

He doesn't know who had spoken. One lone voice.

–Thank you, excellent.

Someone marches up the aisle of the auditorium. Their steps are heavy—whoever it is, trudges like a soldier. He can hear whispering in the back: Avery, giggling with her friends? His new partner is half mounting the stairs when he finally cuts her out of the imposed night-blindness of the stage lights. In her lacy torn black clothes, the nimbus of illumination gives her the glow of a dark angel.

–Eu? –He mouths.

She smiles weakly. –Thought I owed you one, after you so kindly gave me your lunch the other day.

–Alright, please take it from "John, will you sit?"

They take it from there. Ash can only imagine how ridiculously mismatched they look physically—The Giantess and the Beanstalk. He thinks no way will either of them get the part. Maybe Eu thinks that as well, and it's their fatalism that allows them to let go. They read their lines. Then comes the kiss. Clarissa grabs John after he hesitates while trying to tell her his feelings. Eu grabs him. He waits for the regular grip of nausea and the cold sweats, but perhaps he's exhausted and his body can't squeeze out any more terror. This time it doesn't come. His mind is oddly calm. Maybe because it's not real. Maybe because it is real. They move closer. He feels her lips on his; they're soft, she puts her hand behind his head, he buries his in her hair, grips a handful of it. Not too hard. It seems like the natural thing to do. Then his mouth opens; his tongue slips into her mouth, lightly, he doesn't think about it. He feels her long body press against his; they're crushed into each other. They kiss for forty hours and forty days. Dramateacher claps once, to end the scene—the sound is thunder. Something is broken in him and Eu gently pushes him away. He wipes his mouth with the back of his hand.

Eerie silence. Then someone hoots.

People actually *clap*.

–Wow! –Dramateacher is glowing. –Other than that last touch, Mr. Machnik, the two of you had me glued to my seat. Now that's what I mean when I'm talking about chemistry, folks! A fine job! You can go sit down. All right then, Miss Mason, just be prepared that you'll have to read again with your assigned partner. Next up, I have—

They walk down the aisle of the dark theatre and he finds himself following Eu back to where she was sitting, instead of where he was before. He figures he'll get his things later.

–I didn't know you were in this class. –He scribbles a note to her after taking a pencil and a sheet of paper. On stage, the new John fumbles to express himself to the new Clarissa.

–I'm not. –She scribbles back.

–?? –He writes.

–I wanted to try out for the play, but I'm going to miss my class tomorrow. Dentist appointment. Dramateacher told me to come today.

All he writes is: –Oh.

Under the lights, the new Clarissa has just grabbed the new John. Eu watches them kiss, and he watches her watching them: He can see her look in the dark, like an unwrapped present, and she writes again.

–We were way better. :)) BTW, you don't open your mouth for a stage kiss.

He takes the paper, scribbling furiously.

–Sorry. I didn't know.

She writes: –Don't apologize.

He reads it and she takes the paper one last time, then passes it back to him. It says:

–You're a good kisser.

He turns colors.

He wants to tell her she is one too.

He wants to tell her it was his first real kiss.

Ash says nothing.

4

They stand in a shower of hugging girls, staring at the call–back list.

We would like to thank everyone who auditioned! Will the following people please meet in the Fullman Auditorium on Wed. afternoon, for callbacks—

Eu wrinkles her nose.

–Seriously, those two? My dead grammas could've kissed better than they did.

Ash takes the news as par for the course, she makes a last face and then pulls away. They start to walk outside. It's not chronic rain season yet, but the air is chill. He buttons his coat to the top; Eu pulls her trenchcoat close around her.

–The drama club is going to put on the Orestaia in a couple months, I heard, –she says hopefully. –Tragic, bloody Greek theater. Might be more our bag. Anyway, what are you going to do now?

–Go home.

He doesn't offer more. She falls into step with him.

–Oh, ok. I was hoping maybe you were going to stick around for a while. I forgot my key and I can't get into my house until my parents get home later. ...Hey, not to be weird, but do you mind if I go with you?

Ash stumbles.

–...To my house?

–Just to wait until my parents are home. It's cold out here.

No answer comes and she falters. –If it's a problem, no worries. I'll go back to the library or something.

–Uh no. You can come over.

–Really?

–Just to warn you. It's not clean or anything. He looks away.

–I'm sure it's fine. Where do you live?

–The Heights.

Which is a crummy apartment complex not far from their school. It sprawls just behind the main drag, which around that portion of town is a suneaten stretch of strip malls, strip clubs and car dealerships. Before they start walking, he takes out some earbuds, it's not the big headphones today, and he's already put them in when he turns toward her, as if just remembering there's another person around: –Hey, want to share one?

She takes the right one, he the left and they listen to Euro synth pop and bop along the pavement, silently. Eu wouldn't mind talking, but the few questions she asks about when his family moved here and how he likes his new neighborhood are answered in monosyllables. Once they arrive at his complex, he leads her past the screaming, grimy kids out front, through the yard between the saggy two story buildings. The substance under their feet might have once been grass. No wonder this kid's always looking like his cookie broke. Damn, this place is depressing. A pool the color of dirty antifreeze shivers in the corner, and a loud torn banner proudly flops around in the wind by the main office: Now Available! Three Bedrooms! Two Bedrooms! Pool! They wind around on the broken path, dodge a skinny cat, then Ash takes out his key and leads Eu into Unit 32b.

He opens the door, and an undisclosed funk envelops them completely as they step in. The stench is so powerful, Eu's feet freeze for a moment. Rotten food. Indoor smokers. Cat urea. Sweat? *Ugh, not gonna lie, didn't expect Mysterious Fairy Boy to live in such a dump. Don't hold your nose. Do not.* Ash says nothing, only pushes past the kitchen as quickly as possible. In that one glimpse, she sees a sink over-spilling with dirty dishes. The linoleum sags in the middle; life scurries across it. A black shaggy cat perched on the counter leans over the pile, gnawing on some leftovers on one of the plates. It eyes Eu, then keeps on gnawing. They pass the living room and go straight up the stairs—laundry, dirty and maybe clean, litters the narrow stairway. Boxes still everywhere; it looks like much of their stuff is kept in boxes, unpacked. At the end of the hall, Ash directs her into a room.

He steps in behind her, closes the door and Eu is astonished to realize that once they're inside, the smell completely—vanishes. If anything, here it smells pleasant. Faintly of incense. Or candles. There's a bunk bed—the kind with a desk and couch underneath and a bed on top. There are bookshelves set up, of cinderblocks, and the books on it stand carefully ordered. The only stray piece of clothing is a jacket draped on the back of a chair. Ash sits on the chair and motions for her to sit on the couch.

–Ace. Room, –she squeezes out and he makes a face.

–I warned you. This place is awful. I keep my room clean, but that's it. Nobody here cleans up after themselves. –He puts his book bag under the desk and she stretches.

–So your parents are at work?

–They're asleep. They work graveyard so. They tend to stay up for a few hours after they come home, but by then, I'm in school.

–Oh.

They sit and say nothing for a few seconds.

–Do you want something to drink? –he asks abruptly. The silence seems to unsettle him. –I can get you some water, or a coke, or something.

–Sure. I'll have a coke. I can get it myself though...

–Don't bother. I don't want the cat to *attack* you.

He disappears and Eu sits there waiting. One hand travels to her face, starts to pick open a sore on her chin. Bad habit. Her hand drops and her eye travels around the room. Starts to catch on some things. Another desk, in the back corner of the room. Ordered makeup and lotion on the dresser. A spray of boyband and girly anime posters above the bed on top. She can't imagine they were put there by Ash, he seems too gloomy to like such things either ironic– or unironically, but then again, already his apartment is nothing like she imagined. The thought skims through her head. Maybe he shares this room with a younger brother? Maybe he's gay? Maybe both? It would explain a lot. An urge wells up to look in his closet when the door opens. Ash steps back in, with one can of pop and a glass of water. Eu cracks:

–Thanks for ruining my snoop.

He gives her a sharp look, then relaxes his shoulders.

–Snoop away. You won't find anything that great in here.

–If you say so. And? Are you ready for a potentially incendiary question, Ash?

–Incendiary?

Eu looks at him with mock gravity:

–So who did YOU have a crush on back in junior high? Bobby D? Or Niq? The Soulful One. –She starts singing the lines of a cheezy pop single. –*Imma love you, one more time!* C'mon dude, the cameras are off and I know you know the words.

He gives her a dour look and she's already regretting the joke when comprehension breaks over his face.

–Ohhh. You're talking about the boy band posters. That stuff is all my sister's. This is her room too.

–You have a sister?

–Yeah. She goes to our school. I guess you haven't run into her yet.

–I mean, maybe I have and I didn't know.

–You would know if you had. We look exactly like each other. Except, you know, –he mutters awkwardly, –she's a girl.

And you share a room with her, but you're both in high school. That's kinda— Eu doesn't want to embarrass him more though, so she doesn't mention it, turns her attention back to the room instead. The desk by the couch. There's something so pristine about it, even in this pristine room—almost shrine–like. A few pictures carefully tacked onto the wall above, cut out from magazines, all of them black and white. A neat row of sharpened pencils. A pencil sharpener, eraser, ruler and compass. She asks: –So what are you doing here every afternoon, hiding out in your room?'

Ash sits down at the desk.
–Drawing.
–Of course. Do you let people see your pictures?
–No.
–Not even your sister?
–Especially not my sister.
–Well, why not? Are you embarrassed by them?
He's thrown for a moment. Then straightens his back.
–No. I know that I'm good.
–And modest, I see.
Eu grins crooked and he shrugs.
–Literally the only thing I do is draw, and I've been drawing since I was a little kid, so it would be really weird if I wasn't good by now.
–But you still don't show anyone. Why not?
–It's just... it's not going to mean anything to anyone else.
–You can't know that. You should show me.
He says nothing.
–Come on. Please? I won't comment, I won't make fun of it—even if you're drawing fairies, or hentai shit, or Abe Lincolns...
–...Abe Lincolns?
–Yeah. You know, like Mark Ryden.
–...you know Mark Ryden?
–Sure. But my point is, I won't say anything if you don't want me to. I just want to see.
He looks deeply uncomfortable, swallows it, pulls his sketch book from his bag and passes it to her without a word. Eu opens the pages. Angels. Demons. Every-

thing is angels and demons, monsters—dream worlds inhabited by impossibly beautiful, morbid beings. Black and white, veins, sinews, blood, light. Textures. Stones. Tentacles, broken teeth, broken bones. Slime. Nothing she sees in the pages is like anything to be found in real life. She leafs through slowly, savoring the anatomy, the rich, aggressive lines—

–...Do you have more stuff?

–Yeah.

–Really? Can I see?

–If you want. Sure.

He tries to act nonchalant, but she can tell he is excited that she is excited to see his drawings and he brings more sketchbooks, piles them next to her, then tries to busy himself, not wanting to hover too much.

She opens more books.

Bodies, houses, cars, motorcycles, machines, plants, animals, wounds, organs, water. Space, life, death. Color is rare, most of the art is monochrome—ink, and the soot of graphite. Eu wants to run her finger over a drawing and trap the dirt of it on the pad of her finger. She closes the book to resist the temptation, then says to him:

–You know how you draw? –She searches for a moment. –Everything you make is like a dream. You know in dreams, where nothing is really quite 'right'? But it makes perfect sense, in the context of the dream. It's so...

–...So?

–I dunno. It just seems so fluid. So natural. I wish I was this good at something.

Ash shifts from foot to foot.

–You really mean that?

–Dude, you think I'd say something like that if I didn't?

He looks out the window, avoiding her eyes. Eu presses:

–Ash, anybody would say the same, if you bothered to show them. Your parents aren't excited that you can draw this good?

His face hardens.

–They think it's a waste of time. They think what I draw is weird and ugly and that I'd be better off putting my energy into something else.

–Well, they're wrong.

–I know they're wrong. …We used to have huge fights about it when I was younger, but they've pretty much given up. I like to read, and I read a lot, but I'm awful at school, and my grades have always been garbage. I've never been good at anything but drawing, so when I told them I was starting my art school applications, they didn't even say anything.

–Wait, you're looking at… So you're a…

–Junior transfer. I'm seventeen.

–Oh. Same age as me then.

But you don't look it. Eu had assumed Ash was at most, a sophomore. She says: –Well I'm not anywhere as good as all this, but I draw too.

–You do?

–I mean, I just started like last year, but I'm seriously thinking of focusing on illustration or graphic design. I have some sketchbooks, but I haven't been good about filling them. …Maybe we could draw together sometime. I could definitely use the practice.

–Sure. You can come over again and we could draw here if you want. Bring one of your sketchbooks.

–Okay. Just let me know when you're free, I guess.

–I'm always free. Tomorrow?

–Sounds dope as rope.

He smiles, for the second time since she's known him. She leans back against the couch and they talk for the rest of the afternoon. At five, Eu thanks him for letting her stay over and walks home.

4.5

Everyone said Riva Barowicz was a wild card—as if to keep them talking, she ran away to Paris at age 17 with a blond goy artist who promised her the moon and the stars. That's when her mother Rivke started seeing nightmares. In these awful dreams, an angel would come to announce her daughter's death, so she thanked the Creator for never sending her anything more dramatic than dented postcards, scrawled with a hasty line or two. On one of these cards, Riva told her mother to not worry, as she was well on her way to becoming a famous fashion model. Her man had *connections*. On another, Rivke learned that her daughter and him had married. When she read that piece of news, she bit her mouth and it was the only time she could ever remember feeling grateful that her own Lev had died so young. At least he didn't have to see this. She begged her daughter to reconsider; wrote and wrote until her fingers went blue in the face, but it did no good, so against her heart's will, Rivke accepted that her girl was never coming home.

Riva did come back though, five years later—looking tired around the eyes and carting two small children on her narrow hips. The babies glowed, fat and gorgeous, and Rivke forgave her daughter instantly—especially since that good-for-nothing was nowhere to be seen (may he be back in Paris, sleeping on the bottom of the Seine!). The next years rolled by in peace; Riva lowered her head and went to work and the young ones were dumped entirely on Rivke. Not that she minded. When had she been like her changeling daughter? Never: she was so full of energy and hope. The children themselves were bright and obedient and lacking even a drop of their parents' doomed, flashy blood (though the older boy did display an uncanny talent for drawing. Rivke privately wondered if it had to do with being gestated in that debauched western air...) Nonetheless, the two were doing well in their Jewish and regular studies, which is why Rivke fell all but ill when the letters started coming again. What could she do though? Before it had been Paris, now he was making Riva's eyes glister with Beverly Hills stars. He was promising her the American West Coast, and Riva couldn't agree more—isn't that where she belonged? On screens, by poolsides. In mansions. Rivke snorted. Don't think you'll go to America and spend your time in a fancy mansion, or by a pool, sipping coffee! If they ever let you in a mansion, it'll be to clean their toilets! But in her mind, Riva was already overseas. Oh, and she was taking the children too. It was the early 90s, anything was possible. They were going to be a happy, beautiful family. Rivke pleaded, at least leave the young ones, they were doing so well, and they hardly spoke a lick of English! Wouldn't it be better to simply send for them, once everything was settled? (Hoping somewhere deep that in a year, but no more than three, Riva would be back, for good this time.)

But it was no use.

A year later, Riva was living in Cupertino (not Los Angeles, and not Hollywood). Her husband was gone, entranced by a younger muse, and she was alone in California, with some money. Some. Her English was good enough to shack her up with a young American smitten by her sullen good looks (two grade-school kids in tow, or not). He let her know right away though: he wasn't some foreign artiste with disposable income. He could get her work, but none of the jobs would be pretty... So Riva agreed, and worked, and grew older, and let go her dreams. Her taste for glamour wilted. Grew a counterfeit direction and she never contacted her mother again. She knew it was unfair, but it wasn't just that Rivke had been right.

It was that she had been right *twice*.

5.

Eu starts to spend more and more afternoons over at Ash's apartment. His parents she sees practically never; they both work the graveyard shift at the Kingston chemical plant over in M— and are usually asleep in the afternoon. His sister is also never around, dance team and Key Club keep her busy at school. Eu has been going over for three weeks before encountering another member of his family—coming back from the bathroom, she almost runs into a sleepy looking man in their dank hallway, walking barefoot towards the stairs with an unlit cigarette in his hand. He looks Eu over suspiciously, and asks her who she is. When she explains that she is Ash's friend, he contemplates for a moment, nods, claps her on the shoulder and walks past to go down to smoke. Their four second interaction is confusing enough: the guy looks so painfully ordinary. She sees nothing of his son in him.

With Ash, they spend the hours sitting in his room and drawing—he brings her food from the kitchen, and cokes or ice tea, on a tray. He always serves her, refusing to let her go anywhere but the bathroom, as if to protect her from the filth. He apologizes every single time she enters the house for the mess, but Eu gets used to it. Once, she does ask him if he wants to clean up the bottom with her—he tells her that retrograde into disorder is inevitable and leads her upstairs, to draw. She doesn't mention cleaning his apartment again.

When they draw, Eu often uses photographs, or will arrange a still-life on a chair. He draws strictly from his head. They may not move or even talk for hours, but he puts on music in the background—some of it his; some of it hers. They listen to everything, Tool, Bob Dylan, Coltrain, NOFX. Tori Amos, Skinny Puppy, Tracy Chapman, the Offspring, the Cure, Comateens, a-ha, Elvis Costello, Lil Kim, Janis Joplin, Placebo, Wu Tang, Bikini Kill, Michael Jackson, Cindy Lauper, Daft Punk, Rent, Les Mis—old stuff (glam-rock, soul), new stuff (terrorcore, nu-metal).

When they talk, they find out many things about each other.

Ash finds out that Eu's mother Yasmin is a classically trained pianist from Iran, and that she left her parents behind during the Islamic Revolution at the end of the 70s, to come live in America. That her father's brother was already established in the area, running his own instrument repair shop. That's where Yasmin met Eu's father, Harvey (a band teacher at a neighboring local high school and saxophonist). Her oldest brother is touring as a DJ, her middle brother is a roadie, and her younger sister is well on her way to becoming a professional pianist.

In their family, Eu is the odd-one-out; she appreciates music, but has never gotten into making it.

Eu finds out that the guy she ran into in the hall is Ash's stepfather—his real father is who knows where and his extended family lives in Europe. That his teeth are bad, hence the lack of smiling. (More an issue of vanity than of an innate surliness.) That he survives almost entirely off of vitamins, orange soda and orange TicTacs. (Go back to teeth.) And that he hates to be touched. By any person. In any way.

When she casually tries to bring up Ash's eating habits or where his touch phobia comes from, he won't discuss it. He says he's always been like this, that there are some exceptions (certain members of his family and certain stuff his sister makes) and that he's fine.

Eu figures she can respect that. After all, doesn't everyone have those things they don't want to discuss? Only one time does she forget—she comes in for a hug when they're saying goodbye after a lunch break one day and he pushes her away roughly, sweating and embarrassed. They both pretend a second later that nothing happened.

When they walk home from school, boys yell out their car windows at them:

–Hey dyke, your new girlfriend's really pretty.

–Yo Mason. Ask your girl if there are faggots on Mars.

Eu always has a dagger ready on her tongue; he just shoe–gazes.

–C'mon, Ash, –she prompts. –They'll never leave you alone if you always take it.

But his tactic remains trying to stay invisible.

Only in his room does he stretch out to his full size. She asks him once, watching him leaning over his own drawing, happily shading it, what art means to him. Ash shrugs, looks out the window. He says one word:

–Escape.

5.1

When Eu was five, her best friend was the little boy next door (Mark and Joe often froze her out). The last time she ever saw him, he pulled out three dolls when she was at his house—two Barbies and a Ken. The boy told her he'd taken them from his older sister's room. He'd brought outfits too. A scrap of purple plastic for a brush. Eu didn't have Barbies, and it was neat, how you could change the clothes. Switch out the earrings. Style the hair. Maybe she'd ask her mother to buy her one too. Once they divided the outfits and dressed their dolls, they played that Barbie one and Barbie two are best friends, and Ken is Barbie one's husband. Then they played that Barbie one and Barbie two fall in love, kill Ken and bury his body in the desert. The boy told Eu that his sister had a car for them too. Sleek, pink. He'd go to her room and get it. A car would make the desert scene more exciting. While he was looking, his mother came in. Were they hungry? Eu waved a doll at her and said that she was. The mother's mouth turned down. You don't need to bring dolls over, she said. He has so many other toys. I didn't bring them over. He wanted to play with them. Eu didn't understand why the mother got strangely agitated then, or why she got sent home early, or why she was not allowed to go play there again, but her own mother told her not to worry.

She said 'those people are idiots.'

When Eu was seven, a boy at school grabbed the thick ponytail she always wore her hair in and wouldn't let go—he kept pulling and laughing, and snapping it like the reins on a horse, until she turned around and socked him in the face. Swiftly and with zero hesitation. The boy bawled and she was not sorry. The teacher called her parents. Eu's mother told her that she shouldn't have hurt him. But I told him to stop. He wouldn't. Because he was playing. That's how they play with girls they think are pretty. Really, it was a compliment. Eu's father told her it was good that she had punched him.

When Eu was ten, a girl at school who was two years older told her that she looked like an immigrant and that she should 'go back to where you came from.' Eu pushed her to the ground and some knees got skinned bloody. The teacher called her parents. Her mother said the girl had deserved what she'd got. Her brothers said Eu was tough and after that, they let her hang out with them much more.

When Eu was eleven, she asked her brothers to shave off all her hair. Mark and Joe did it to be funny, and their mother almost fainted when she came home that night from work. "Boys will think you're ugly! They'll make fun of you!" She wailed. Only one boy was foolish enough to do this: she punched his lights out. The teacher called her parents, and Eu got suspended. Her mother said she deserved it, for making herself look freakish. Her father said, it was good that she was standing up for herself. But she should tone it down. After that, she got a reputation in school for being a trouble maker and her star as the Resident Scary Bitch began to rise.

This made Eu happy.

When Eu was thirteen, her mother gave her a razor. And told her she needed to start shaving her armpits, and legs, and arms, and mustache, and that she should pluck the hair between her eyebrows. She hadn't inherited her father's sandy, light hair, and now it was her turn to keep fighting the legacy of hairiness. Boys didn't like girls with wooly arms and legs, and mustaches. Her father didn't like it either, that's why her mother kept going to the waxing salon! But Eu was too young to go waxing. Maybe when she was older... until then, she could just shave. And pluck. Eu listened to her mother patiently, then threw the razor in the garbage once she was alone again. Thinking, hmm, boys sure were finicky! They didn't like if you were hairy. They also didn't like if you swore, smoked, ate a lot, and wore a lot of black. But Eu loved all of those things—and too bad she'd never gotten the memo stating that boys are essential creatures whose whims are *important*.

If anything, the older she got, the more certain she was: Boys and men were born to be shunned.

When she was fourteen, a girl she was working on a project with asked her to go see a movie together. When the girl took her hand in the movie theatre, naive Eu realized, she hadn't just been asked out. She had been asked *out*. She liked the girl well enough, but she liked the rumors that started spreading about her at school even more. Her girlfriend Elani was rather short and slight, so they generally left her alone, but Eu was already taller than many guys. So they said she was a dyke. The way they'd spit the word, she knew they were trying to hurt her, but the effect was quite the opposite. *Good, the smoothbrains are finally getting it.* She wasn't here for boys. She wasn't meant for boys.

As if she'd be caught dead, pandering to some asinine boy!

Never. Never.

5.2

It's the Wednesday of the fifth week since she first came over. Eu looks up from Ash's couch. The clock says 3:47. He's furiously shading something at his desk—she's stippling the side of a lemon, next to an empty bottle and a dried flower. An ice cold can of coke sweats next to her and Thom Yorke's spectral voice haunts the background.

The afternoon is floating and perfect.

–Hey Ash.

–Yeah?

She stares at the lemon now, letting herself get distracted by its rich bumpy skin, then suddenly looks up at his bookshelf. *The Neuromancer. The Hitchhiker's Guide to the Galaxy. Dune. The Clockwork Orange. Ender's Game. Wraeththu.*

Her eye stops. She stands up, pulls the book out.

–Yeah? –He's still looking at her.

Eu's mind muddles.

–Nice books... malchik.

–Those two shelves are mine. You can take that one if you want. ...devotchka.

She stares at her own hands, mid–pull, as if she had forgotten what she'd been doing.

–*Wraeththu*, huh? I read this book, years ago. Did you ever get to reading it?

–Yeah.

–My aunt got it for me for my birthday one year, she knew I liked fantasy and didn't really look into if it was "age appropriate." I remember the author describing the beautiful Wreaththu guys having their amazing magic sex and impregnating each other and my twelve year old mind was so fucking BLOWN, you know?

A beat. He puts his pencil down carefully.

–...You wanted to talk to me about Wreaththu sex?

She clears her throat, carefully pushes the book back on the shelf.

–No. Actually what I wanted to ask was. well, do you have a girlfriend?

Ash narrows his eyes.

–Sure. Girls are just lining up to be with someone who has to puke every time they come near him.

–Hey. It was a serious question.

–Well, we're hanging out all the time. Don't you think you'd know by now? If I did?

–I guess. Well anyway, I was thinking about your touch thing. I looked it up in the library the other day. I didn't know it's called...

–Aphephobia. –His tone is hollow. –Or aphenphos-mphobia.

–And have you ever seen someone about it or tried to do anything about it?

–...

–I was thinking, maybe you need to be more *pro-active*. You're not comfortable around people, you don't like people touching you and— maybe being with some-one could ease that out. Haven't you ever wanted to at least see if you could do something about it?

He picks up his pencil and shades aggressively.

–...No girl has ever wanted to go out with me. So I don't think I have to worry about it.

God, is this proof I'm not actually a girl?

Eu breathes deep.

–Listen Ash, I mean, we're getting along well, and I'm always over anyway and I know about your thing, so I would never pressure you to... you know. –Her ears start to burn –So anyway, what I'm trying to say, badly, is that I was thinking, well. You know. ...that maybe I could be your girlfriend.

Because I think I might be meant to be with someone who brings me cokes and draws like a dream and listens to Thom Yorke and is just an absolute—

The tip of his 3B pencil snaps. He sharpens it quickly and drives the fresh graphite down onto the paper with a renewed ferocity.

Lord in Heaven, fuck me like you draw a picture.

Eulalie Nour Mason, what the actual fucking fuck is wrong with you?

Will you ALL just shut up, he's ANSWERING.

Ash indeed starts saying something, or at least, attempting to.

–Eu uhh. –He seems to have trouble talking too. –Uhm, I'm really glad we've become close friends. Really, I never thought I'd have a friend like you, uhh, ever, but well, there's already someone I like. At school.

Ok dude, do us all a fucking favor and DO NOT ask him who it is. He won't tell you anyway unless you ask, and trust me, you don't want to know. It's either going to be some ridiculously pretty and boring girl with HUGE tits, demonstrating his utterly pedestrian goofy male taste, or even WORSE, a ridiculously pretty and actually cool and funny girl you could never compete with, so just keep moving your pencil keep it moving RIGHT along, don't you DARE open your fat mouth and...

Ask him, faggot.

–So who is it?

Eu takes a deep breath and internally screams for ten years. Ash's neck stiffens.

–You really want to know?

–Did I ask?

He puts his pencil down, finally turns around.

A pregnant pause.

–Eric Swenson.

He turns back, picks up his pencil and resumes shading, without waiting for her response or reaction. And it does take some seconds for Eu to recover.

Well, damn.

Eric Swenson is the first son of a family descended from Nordic immigrants. He has the body of Adonis; the popularity of JFK, and is simultaneously cherished as the darling of the swim team and of the AP math program. It takes her a good five seconds to formulate a response.

–Well, well. Never pegged you for a tryhard.

–Come on, Eu. I can't help it if I like him.

–So does eighty percent of the female student body, so you have enough competition. But good luck.

–Whatever. I don't think he's into guys anyway.

–You never know until you ask. I mean, I had no idea you were into trophy boys.

Or boys in general.

She thinks of delicate Ash next to brawny Eric and the picture is almost ludicrous. And hypocritical, because if she's honest with herself, she's probably even taller than Eric.

Come on, Eu. You really gonna sit there and act

shocked? The kid's warmer than a fucking PopTart, and you already speculated that, so now he's just confirmed it, and you're mad. What for? Because the little wanker's aiming waaaay out of his league? Or.

Maybe she's the one aiming out of her league. Maybe Ash is a trophy boy too. She suddenly remembers an ongoing dialogue conducted through the media of bathroom wall in stall two of the southern hall's bathroom she had noticed last week. Miss Platt had just gotten herself revved up about the Stamp Act when Eu had excused herself. If she ever did this, she liked to go to the bathroom when nobody was around, during class. *I always overdo it, and then my stomach feels so heavy and gross.* She made sure the bathroom was empty, locked herself in the last stall and was dealing with her issues sitting on the toilet when right next to the dispenser, she discovered a surprising thread on the wall:

Boys I wanna fuck:
Joe F.
And you?
It asked future urinators.
Her eye traveled down the list.
First name. Eric S.
Then, in pink gel–pen came the line
James Torrez = hot!!!
The final addition to the wishlist, in ballpoint—
A. Machnik.
Her stomach churned harder than ever.
You don't say.
But that wasn't all.

An arrow pointed from his name to a new message in hasty pencil:

Ewww whyyy? He looks like a GIRL. :/

Ballpoint came back: Only his FACE : >

Someone else: So, cover it?

A rando blue pen: He's a fag.

There it is, she thought then. She wondered how something as complex as a human being could be reduced to a few lines like that. Stripped. Eu was embarrassed for him and if she had an eraser, or a pen, she would have gone back and scratched out the whole message, but nothing could've scratched out what she herself was thinking:

That Asher Machnik had a face that could stop traffic. If he was a girl. As a boy though, all it did was disorient people. Her especially.

Sitting in his room now, she looks up at him. His pencil is still down and his eyes flash.

–He's not a trophy boy, OK? Whatever that even is. He helped me out a lot the first few days of school, when he really didn't have to. Not everyone who's popular has to be an evil bastard, you know.

–Sure, –she says, disliking Eric Swenson even more. Not only is he beautiful, but he has to be nice. She cruelly wonders if Ash is one of those socially beaten people who falls in love with the first person to show him kindness. Too bad then that Eric beat her to the punch. But her one–word answer just fuels his anger:

–Do you have a problem with it? You can tell me straight up if you're closed–minded.

She spits, –You honestly think I give two shits if

you're *warm?* If you want to know, I happen to consider myself bi. I was just surprised, is all. You could've said something earlier.

–What, like, "Hi, my name's Ash and I like a guy?" I didn't think it was important enough to bring up if it didn't come up.

–Fine. Just forget it.

–See? I knew you would react like this. –His tone is sulky and poisonous and Eu recoils angrily.

–Oh, knock it OFF. I'm just bitter, I'm not a bigot, for all I care, you can *marry* Eric Swenson and have a pile of beautiful babies with him. In fact, I hope you do.

–Maybe I will.

–Great.

–Great.

It's their first fight. Both of them scribble in angry silence and Eu is surprised to feel tears in her eyes. To make matters worse, the door suddenly opens.

–Oh. Hi.

Lena Machnik stares at Eulalie Mason; Eulalie Mason stares at Lena Machnik. She quickly brushes the tears away, hoping nobody noticed, then stands up. Ash stands too.

–Hey Lena. This is my friend from school I told you about. Eulalie. Eu, this is my sister. I guess you haven't met yet?

Lena has the usual flicker of surprise strangers get over their face when they first take in the elements that make up Eulalie Mason: The raw-boned height. Aggressive features. The strange name. The strange clothes. Eu has the usual surprise flicker over hers from seeing the siblings together for the first time. They look startlingly alike, right down to the slight divet in their chin, except, as he had said once, that Lena is a girl. She has thick, slippery honey-colored hair she flicks over her shoulder constantly and a willowy runway frame that stops just an inch short of Ash's. Eu doesn't want to, but she hates her immediately.

What the fuck were their parents eating when they made these two? Holy shit.

Out loud, she mumbles:

–Sorry for invading your room like this.

Even her smile is like his. Warm and mouth closed.

–Oh, you're fine. I'm just grabbing something and leaving anyway. I'm hardly ever in here. Ash, we baked cookies at Trina's and I brought some over in a tupperwear. If you two are hungry, go ahead and have some.

Great, another beautiful, nice person.

Lena runs over to her brother and they hug with the intensity of a couple reunited on a train platform. Lena whispers something to him and Eu feels oddly uncomfortable in their presence, because the Ash she knows is physically and emotionally remote. To say the least. Now he seems so happy, he's even forgotten that Eu is here. The air is tense and unsettling, she almost gets up to leave, but his sister had already grabbed a textbook from the drawer of the other small desk and is stuffing it into her bag. She won't stay longer than a minute.

–Will you be back for dinner? –Ash asks her.

–No. So, I made you a plate. Please eat some? It's covered in the fridge. Just heat it up. I have to finish that video with Trish so I'm going to eat at her house.

–OK. Is her mom giving you a ride home?

–No, she's at her aerobics thing tonight.

–All right. Then call me twenty minutes before you're done and I'll walk over to pick you up. I don't want you walking home alone that late.

–Thanks. I'll call you later then.

Lena hoists her bag onto her shoulder and raises to her full height—

–Alright. Bye bye. ...Nice to meet you. –She nods back at Eu, then turns, walks over to where Ash is sitting. She says something to him in a foreign language. He smiles, and says something back to her in that language—Lena leans down.

They kiss each other on the lips.

...It's not exactly a peck, either.

Then she leaves.

Ash turns back down to his paper, pushes hair out of his eyes and resumes drawing.

They don't talk.

Eu thinks:

Don't try to process it all. One thing at a time.

She's burning to ask if kissing his little sister on the lips is some kind of regular thing, or if it was a one-time performance, trotted out for her own personal consternation, but she doesn't want to add more oil to the fire.

Instead, she says carefully: –I'd never heard you speak Russian before. That was Russian, right?

–Yeah. I told you we lived outside ______ with my grandmother until I was ten. Or did I keep that from you too?

Yup, he's still mad at me.

–Ash look, I'm sorry.

–For judging me?

–Dude, I was not judging you!

–You know, you're the first person I've ever told about him. Or about...anyone... like that. This is another reason why my parents don't like me drawing.

–What are you talking about?

His tone is leaden. –Forever they've been saying that someone who spends all their time drawing gives off a ...you know. A certain *vibe*. They're always on me about how I dress and how I look and well... I never let them pressure me into pretending I like sports, or anything, but yeah... It looks like I like a guy, so I guess they were right about me, all along.

Guilt rolls over Eu.

–Look dude, anybody who doesn't like your vibe is missing out! Anyway, it's not like I don't understand. I used to date this girl. Back in freshman year...

–You did?

–Why do you think everyone at school's always calling me a dyke? I haven't been with anyone since then, but sure, once people make up their mind, they won't shut up. Anyway... I'm sorry I reacted like that. I got the wrong idea. It's not your fault and it's nobody's business who you like or don't like, it's just that we've been spending so much time together and then—

Don't say it.

She says it.

–Then there was that kiss at school.

Ash gives her a look as if she were insufferably naïve.

–Eu, that kiss? Was ACTING.

Then you really should have gotten the role of John, she can't help but think to herself. *Because you are one damn good actor.*

6.

586 jaws are moving up and down. It's second lunch; the biggest lunch period at their school, and the entire room buzzes with teeth churning to annihilate French-fries, Frito-Lays, turkey sandwiches and fruit roll ups. His jaw is one of the few not moving; it rests lightly against his right hand; his left hand grips a mechanical pencil and drifts over his sketchbook. Usually he listens to music, but today even that is distracting. He keeps going back to it. Eu's sudden confession, his hasty explanation of Eric (did he even have a crush on Eric? He may as well have had a crush on the sun) and the subsequent mess. The entire rotten cherry-on-top—Lena coming in. He'd become so comfortable around Eu, he hadn't even thought to think about—he shivered. The closest he'd ever come to having a friend who wasn't his sister and now maybe, it was all gone. Because he was a monster. Or at least, someone who needed serious help—

Eu sinks onto the bench next to him.

–Still chuffed, Ash-baby?

He glances over at her.

She looks like she always looks, happy to see him and up to no good and he paints over his relief by rolling his eyes and closing his book.

–I was never chuffed. Does that word mean pissed? If it does, then you were chuffed, because I like some guy who doesn't even know I exist.

–Then it's agreed: Truce.

She reaches out her hand, remembers and pulls it back and without further ado, starts rummaging through his lunch-bag and he smiles. Her appetite never ceases to amuse him.

–Ugh, you have to tell your mom to stop making you egg salad.

–Lena makes my lunch; not my mom. But sure, I'll pass it on.

–She lives in your room, she makes your lunch; what else does your hot baby sister do for you?

Sometimes, Eulalie really wishes she could punch herself in the face. She blanches white—

Ash's lips press into a hard line.

–You have two seconds to take that back.

–I'm sorry. Really, I don't know what the hell is wrong with me. Just seriously, pretend I said nothing. Will you do that? Because I came with a peace-offering.

–Funny way you have of showing it.

–Look, I said I was sorry! Oh gosh, my geesh! Want me to cut off my head in apology to you?

–What is it then?

He rolls his eyes again, and he wants to keep being mad, or try to explain any of that situation to her, but then she starts to eat.

Eu unwraps the Hostess cupcake as gently as a girl undressing another girl and her black eyes narrow mischievously—

–Why are you looking at me like that? –She asks him, teeth still poised to bite.

–Like what?

–I dunno, like you enjoy watching me eat.

His face runs a high color.

–Is it weird?

–Not weirdweird, but cuteweird—

–Well, that's how I feel like when I see you eat. I think how much you like food is... cuteweird.

Eu snorts.

–Tell that to my mom. I can't rattle a chip bag without her telling me I need to lay off the food. But hey, let's not stray off topic. –She bites into the cupcake, flutters her eyelashes appreciatively then draws out two tickets from her trenchcoat pocket. –Tralaaa!

–What's that?

–Tickets to see the Killahz this weekend. Them and Muftie, a band you've never heard of, I'm sure, but that you'll love. The venue sucks balls, it's the London, but the music is going to be *ace*.

–The London is?

–This crusty, gross little club my brother used to take me to when he first started DJ-ing. You'll adore it.

–So like... a dance club? –He says 'dance club' like 'alligator pit'. –But I don't dance.

–Ash, can you STOP being such an antisocial little *morphodite*?? You'll *long* to dance when you hear them, you'll see! And going out will be good for you. Say you'll come. Pweeeaaaase.

She has more cake while she waits for his response, and her eyes roll back in her head and she lets out a lascivious moan. Someone at the table next to them turns around and stares, Eulalie makes a rude gesture at them, and Ash smirks.

–Sure, –he says finally. –How can I refuse, when you ask while giving head to my food?

–That's the spirit! I mean, what's the worst that can happen?

He ticks on his fingers. –Other than having a huge panic attack and maybe puking on a total stranger?

–That won't happen. I'll be there to watch out for you.

He wants to tell her that panic attacks don't work like that, but he can't deny, he's curious. He has never gone out with anyone before. Other than with Lena, or being a chaperone for her and her friends when she was younger, but that didn't count. He wonders what it's like to go out. And if he could handle it. Eu shoves the rest of the cake into her face, makes an impressive three point shot with the sandwich into the garbage can across the cafeteria and starts to peel his banana.

–I'm guessing you don't know where the London Theatre is?

–No.

–Ok. I'll give you the address later. I can't come over until the concert—I've got to finish this essay for my German class by Friday, just stab me.

He's so happy that everything is still okay between them, that he almost suggests that she still come over and do homework at his place instead of drawing. He stops himself though, not wanting to come off as clingy.

–Sure. Then I'll meet you at the club before the concert.

–Great. By the way. –She runs her tongue over the tip of the banana suggestively and raises an eyebrow at him. –There are going to be a lot of cute boys there. Cute enough to make you forget that boring ol' straight-o Eric Swenson. So dress *hot*.

7

Ash gets off the bus and turns right, following the crude map Eulalie had drawn him. At one point, he is unsure if he is going the right direction; this is an industrial part of town and it's hard to spot any building numbers. He sucks on an orange sucker while he looks around, pretty sure he must be close—

Behind him, someone yells from a car.

–Hey babe, you lost? I think we got what you're looking for, right here.

God, not now; on the bright side, he finally sees a number on a building further down, yes, he is heading the right way.

He starts to walk faster, ignoring that the car has started slowly driving next to him.

–Tell us where you're going. We'll give you a ride.

–...

–What's wrong? Too good to talk to us?

–...

–Turn around.

An obnoxious blare of car horn. BLAAAAP!

–C'mon babe, turn around!

Ash turns to face the car, draws his slouch up to his 5'11" height and slowly pulls the sucker out of his face. Narrows his eyes.

Turns back and continues striding down the street.

The driver starts cackling—

–Oi, help me out here. I'm confused. Is it a chick trying to be a dude, or a dude trying to be a chick?

–Fucking FREAK!

Sweat beads at his hairline, but he doesn't slow down. The passenger throws a half can of pop out at him as the car screams past, but he dodges it, right before he sees that he's arrived at the right spot.

There's the alley, as marked. He walks down and hears the reassuring sound of people buzzing. Near the end of the alley a giant metal door is propped open; a group of people congregates outside, talking and laughing. Eu stands to the side and he takes in her outfit before she has a chance to notice him: shit kickers, tight black pants ripped every which where, a tight black tank top that fits snugly over her upper body. The bandages underneath the top. A loose open shirt over all. Her dark hair is tied in a vicious knot at the nape of her neck and she's wearing an army of bracelets. He thinks she looks good. When she sees Ash, she excuses herself from her friend, and scampers over to him. He's surprised that a girl of her stature can move so gracefully at times.

–Hey. You found it.

–Thanks to your map.

She looks him over with appreciation.

–Nice. I see you took my dress-code warning seriously. You look ...ultra.

–Ultra... what?

Eu wants to kiss him on the cheek. Doesn't.

–Just ultra. Come on.

They go into the club. The London Theatre. It's a place that Eu used to come to a lot when her older brother was still playing smaller gigs; now that he's touring big venues, she's stopped going regularly, but she still has some friends working in the back as sound boys—a couple of her brother's old friends in the bar. Occasionally she'll stop in for a free show, or if someone she especially likes is playing. The music is varied, live or DJs, ska, electronic—tonight, most people will come to hear The Killahz, though she was telling him earlier that the opening band is by far the better, and great for dancing.

She pulls him down into the main area, past the hellishly lit coat-check. The dance area is the regular black-box tomb—ghosts float around the edges, drinking or smoking, though the group seems to be rather mixed. Eu shows him where he can stow his coat, takes him over to the bar and they sit on the wobbly patched stools and drink bitter lemon.

–Nice dog-collar. –She nods at the ring hanging from his neck. He doesn't tell her that it's a memento from the only dog they'd ever had. Lena especially had loved that dog, and so she kept his collar in her box of Important Things. But he had been wondering desperately what someone wears to a rock show, and he figured that it might fit. And he'd done his makeup. He was glad Lena was gone for the afternoon—it's not that he was ashamed of putting on makeup (he'd done it in front of her, too), but he'd never left the house with it on before. She would have been grilling him about where he was going out, dressed like that.

Eu says: –Your makeup is killer. I guess you could never do your face up for school and live to tell the tale.

–Not likely.

–So, you want to drink something else? Something a little... stronger? I know the bartender, he'll give me beer if I ask.

–If you're having one.

–Wait, have you ever even had a drink before?

–At holidays, sure. My parents let me have wine.

–Just one then. I'm only having one too.

She goes to get the beers, and he sees her fall into conversation at the end of the bar. He watches her talking to the bartender easily, and wonders what it would be like to go into a club, to know everyone at the door, at the bar, backstage. With nobody around him, he has time to sit back and take it all in. It's not much anything like what he had been expecting. No sleek acres of neon and lights and bodies pushing against each other—that's what he'd been afraid of when she'd first said 'club', those frenetic cybernetic spaces they show in movies. Here, it's dark, almost shabby—with plenty of people but also plenty of space. Eu is still talking, Ash's eyes continue to wander around the room, and he's thinking—she wasn't lying when she talked about the boys. The place is populated with the kinds of people he never thought existed in real life. His gaze comes to a rest: an older guy with icewhite hair is standing across the room and smiles when he catches him staring. Ash keeps looking, almost smiles back, then casts his eyes down. When he dares to look up again, the guy is still looking—then starts to walk over.

Ash glances back at Eu, she is still occupied. The stranger slides into her empty seat with the confidence of very attractive people who are unaccustomed to rejection.

He wonders if he's lost his mind, staring so openly like that. Shoots a desperate look at the bar; Eu is not moving, so he summons every fiber in his body to stave off a meltdown as the stranger greets him.

–Hey.

–H-hi.

–Cheers. Never seen you around here before.

–It's my first time. Here. My first time here.

–I got what you meant. –The guy grins. –So, you always stare like that?

–I'm sorry, –he stammers. –I th-th-thought I was just staring into space. Not at you.

–That's too bad.

–What?

–I mean, I was happy you were staring at me, but if I'm not your thing, I can leave you alone...

–No, no! You are my thing. I mean...

God, you are sounding like a complete mess.

The stranger however seems to be enjoying his mess.

–So that girl who was sitting here with you earlier. ...You with her?

The question rubs him strange, but he answers.

–I mean, I'm with her here... tonight.

–But she's not your girlfriend?

–No.

–Yeah, I didn't think so. –The guy smiles. His teeth are perfect. All of him is perfect. –My name's Nick. You are?

–Ash.

He extends his hand and when Ash shakes it, he feels the rush of nausea envelop him. Pulls away as quickly as he can, but his palms are already throbbing and wet. Internal panic spreads.

I cannot do this. I don't belong here. Why did I think I could do this? Eu, please come back. Please. Please.

Nick is still smiling at him.

–You look... on edge. Everything good?

Ash takes a deep breath.

–Yeah. I just uhh... I'm not used to...

–You're not used to the whole scene. I understand. Can I get you a drink?

–My f-friend is getting us drinks right n-now... but t-thanks.

–Can I get you something else then?

Nick looks at him like he is supposed to know what that means. Ash raises an eyebrow, and Nick takes out a small tin box. Flicks it open. He uses a fingertip to pick up one of the tiny pills and puts it on his own tongue.

–Are you interested?

–What does it do?

–Nothing bad. You'll just see a nice dream. And it'll help you relax.

Ash's hand shakes. *He knows that he shouldn't.*But he looks over and thinks Nick may have the bluest eyes he's ever seen.

His heart is in his throat. He doesn't say anything, but the other has picked up another pill on the tip of his finger and extends it towards him questioningly. Ash closes his eyes. He imagines himself, feeling relaxed. He imagines himself, feeling at ease. He opens his mouth. Feels something on his tongue, feels Nick's fingertip on his lower lip.

He swallows the pill and then Nick gets up, smiling.

–See you on the floor, Ash, –he says.

And disappears.

8.

Muftie blares on stage; they're doing a rowdy cover of Placebo's "Nancy Boy" and Eu and Ash are just two bodies in a tangle of sweating kids, screaming, jumping and careening around. Deep in the crush of dancers, though not quite at the mosh pit's core—occasionally a person in a sweaty T-back is bulldozed against them and they happily shove them back into the cloud of churning bodies colliding like over-excited molecules. Some people are crowd surfing and they have to watch out for the occasional steeltoed Doc flailing at a dangerous temple-height. Eu wonders if she's ever seen Ash look this carefree—he's even *dancing*, okay, not particularly well, but then none of the people here are—everyone moves in some feverish output of energy that is much too chaotic to be really dancing. Just a release of pent-up joy, frustration, and physical rage.

Ash himself is wondering if he's ever felt this good before. Vivid colors stream off the stage and he's bathed in them, steaming in them, tasting the sounds, hearing the smells of sweat, perfume, and pot. He's used to feeling overwhelmed by bad sensations—this is so different. Every person pushed into him makes his skin crawl deliciously.

Every boy and girl looks dangerously attractive.

–Eu, did I tell you how good you look tonight?

No, she thinks, blushing all over, and he grabs her, laughing, and starts to spin her around. They spin faster, and she trips against someone, apologizes, he leans his head against her shoulder. Being loud, grabbing her hands, hugging her tight—perfectly normal behavior for a kid in a club and perfectly abnormal behavior for Ash. She honestly had no idea how the night would turn and was equally prepared to bail early, or for Ash to have some fun, but this is more than she even dreamed to hope for. Was it the drink?

–Come on, –she teases him –you cannot be this fucked up after one beer!

He shakes his head, giggling and almost falls down.

–Jesus H. Baldheaded Christ! You really are a lightweight!

She gently pulls him upright, and it's the first time it comes into her head. That something's not right.

–Ash, are you okay?

It's not inconceivable that one drink would affect him so much, she figures. He is very skinny. *Or maybe he took something from someone while I was gone.* She can't imagine it though. In all their conversations, he's never once talked about using drugs or wanting to, even when she's talked about using them—

Ash smiles. –I'm fine! I'm just having fun. This is a great band. I like this whole eighties thing they've got going—did you check out the guy's guitar?

She looks at it, and when she looks back, a small group has joined them. Eu doesn't know them, though one of them seems to know Ash—a tall guy, unjustly handsome, college age, if she had to say. Maybe even older. His hair is bleached the color of glass and his eyes are an almost unnatural ice blue. He's talking to Ash, flirting with him, and she can see her friend practically melt under the guy's attention. Finally, the group moves away.

She whispers: –Dang. I think that's the first time I've seen someone make you lose your shit.

He blushes. Eu says,

–Hey, no worries. He is extremely cute. And he obviously thinks you are. Did you see his pants though? Woof, tight enough to tell his religion.

–Stop.

–What? It's true. Don't act like you didn't notice. That he's definitely not a Jew...

Ash says nothing, just grins and grabs her hand again. Starts to spin her.

The band rages, something rages in her too. The feel of his hands; his grip is firm and not something she normally gets to feel; she's gotten used to being kept at arm's length, but not tonight—tonight, he keeps hugging her, rubbing her shoulder, grabbing her hand, petting her hair. Eu wonders if it's the combination of the beer and the sweaty euphoria of the dancers. They cling to each other and spin, screaming—anytime they knock into someone else, which is all the time, Ash laughs.

–Your face is really red, –she says to him then, and he touches it. Oddly, he starts to stroke his own face, as if feeling it for the first time.

–I guess so. I guess I could go wash it in the bathroom.

–Maybe you should splash some water on it.

–Sure. Will you be here when I come back?

–Where else would I be?

He bends down and gently kisses her on the hand, between her thumb and index finger, and Eu tenses. Right now, she feels like she could get him to do more than that; she could even kiss him again, like they did on stage, but something about his state makes her not want to. She watches him go towards the bathroom, then someone taps her on the shoulder—it's an old club friend of hers, Clara. They talk.

9.

Ash jiggles the men's room doorknob for twenty breaths before his blurred vision focuses on the sign above him:

> *Out of Order. Y'all have to go to the ladies!*
> *–London Management*

So he falls into the ladies room next door.

The inside of the female restroom is painted an evil, absolute red—red as congealed blood, the ceilings, walls and couch—the mirror is scrawled with graffiti, as are the walls, and wallpapered in the stickers of bands long disbanded. He stands in the middle of a huge, defiled cherry and can almost see the color dying into him. A pretty goth girl and boy are at the long mirror, pressing their lips and applying eyeliner; Ash stumbles by and splashes water on his face from the sink. He tries to dry his hands, but there are no paper towels; they are already strewn all over the floor, brewing in a combination of water, spilled drinks, and pee. He's too high to be disgusted though, examines the stew under his boots with an almost clinical attention, when he feels someone tap him on the shoulder.

–Hey.

He turns. Nick is behind him, smiling.

–Hi Nick.

If it's at all possible, Nick looks even more attractive than he did before. He stands against the wall, close to Ash, with another boy with deep brown hair. Both in tight, black jeans. Studded belts. Nick reaches over and fingers his dog-collar.

–You remembered my name.

–Of course.

–So, seeing any nice dreams yet?

–Sure...

–That's good, –he says.

Runs a finger down his neck—and Ash feels the touch sear straight through his skin. His entire body burns. He leans into the hand, like a cat getting stroked. Nick massages him and his hands go down to his shoulders; lightly pushes Ash against the wall, and the pressure of his petting feels so good and warm, Ash has to bite his tongue to not moan out loud. The other guy steps over and begins slowly kissing him. Nick rubs his shoulders and back—the boy and the girl at the sinks steadily apply their makeup while watching in the mirror with the detached interest you give to street performers.

Nick touches him everywhere and liquefies him; everything in him aches. The other guy sucks on his neck, Nick unzips his pants. That's when something negative registers, but in that overwhelming fog it's so hard to think clearly.

Aaaaahn. Aaaaaah. Who's making that noise? Oh, I guess it's me, that's weird I didn't think people actually moaned in real life, I thought that's just something they do in porn, but you can't really help it can you, this feels so good, kind of strange but good, these guys like me, they want me, they don't think I'm some kind of freak, oh but you ARE a freak, why do you think those other people in the bathroom are staring at you? you shouldn't BE in here like this, shut up please, shut up and let me like it for once, it's not Eric at school, it's not anyone anybody is ever going to know about, so I don't have to worry about anything or feel bad about anything and I can just like it for once... Ash, do you even know these guys' names? Of course I do, the one kissing me is Nick and the other one is... He's... Noname is taking your belt off, that's fine, that feels so aaa, they're not going to stop there, you know that right? Good, I don't want them to stop. I'm sick of being scared of this, I'm sick of always doing it alone, let someone else do it for a change, that's not all they want though, they want to, that's fine, what-ever they want, I want it too—

Whatever they want, I want it too.

You want it right, Ash? You want it, right?

Answer me, Ash.

Answer me, Ash. Yes or

–No, –he moans weakly, pushes against them, and Nick pets his head:

–You don't want to out here?

Maybe that's what his no meant.

Ash is not sure.

Nick nods, he pushes open one of the empty stalls and stuffs Ash into it. The other guy comes behind them and they latch the door. In the stall to the right someone flushes and leaves—in the stall to the left someone's tak-ing a dump.

Ash is up against the wall—both Nick and the other guy stroke him now, sometimes they kiss him, sometimes each other. He's too messed up to do anything back to them, but a hand runs through his hair, grips it; the sensation tingles his skin all over. He's sweating—the moisture runs down his neck, his back. He's scared; and it's a vague fear he can't fully identify. Odd, because he knows a thousand colors of fear. But this particular shade is new. Nick pulls down Ash's pants, unzips his own. Ash hears the crinkle of a wrapper, something drips onto him from the back: cold.

The other guy speaks: –Hey, maybe you should stop. He looks scared and he's sweating like crazy.

–He's fine, –Nick kisses Ash on the back of his neck.

–Careful man, he's just a kid. You're going to hurt him.

–I'm not. You're good, right Ash? I'm not going to hurt you. You want me to?

–Dude, he's not saying 'yes.'

–Well, he's not saying 'no' either.

Nick presses the length of his body from behind, slick, aggressive, and Ash doesn't know what to say. The truth is, he does want him to, but not here and not like this, and his mind feels so hot and dull. Suddenly, Eu appears behind his eyes. She always seems to know what to say and do in any situation and he wishes then that he'd hear the bathroom's front door bang open—hear her mercenary clomp so he could call out to her, but she's not here, and she's not coming, and the necessary steps to make this all stop seem tremendously complicated.

Resigned, Ash turns his face into the wall

And says nothing.

.

Breathe. Breathe. Breathe. Breathe.
And then...

He thinks

You ever felt pain this bad?

N

o

So this is sex.

No...
This cannot be it.

Flush (toilet)
Laughter
Laughter
Bang (stall door)

Ash concentrates on a name carved into the wall .25 inches from his face.

I love Annika.

I love Annika.

I love Annika.
Help me, Annika.

Nick pulls on his dog collar so hard, he starts
coughing.
The other guy watches with pity, finally, gets on his
knees next to him and starts to...
Ash grips the toilet paper dispenser harder.

*Now I know none of you are going to recognize this
next number, because we wrote this on the road two
months ago while Cole was on his hiatus. We really wanted to play it for you tonight though, because it's when we
wrote this song that we realized—*

And the crowd goes

When he loses himself listening to the band is
when he realizes: something in his numbed body has
turned insidiously.

Alone, he's often tried to prolong the moment by
concentrating, but here it is impossible to focus. All he
can do is pretend it's not happening.

The guy on his knees grips his lower leg.

Fuck, that is a LOT. Kid, you could've warned me.
Haha, told you...ahhh... that he wanted to.
Shut the fuck up, man.

Ash bites his own tongue hard.
Blood spreads in his mouth.

Nick, you done soon? I wanna catch the next song—

Y–eah I just...

And then and then—
The extraction hurts about as much as the insertion.

Ash still on the wall, face turned, one cheek against
the scarred surface.
It's over.It's over.
It's over.It's over.
Nick is closing his belt—

                                          You good?

You good?

Y o u   g o o d ?

It takes Ash nine seconds to register that he's being
talked to.

He nods dully.
For the first time, Nick looks unsure
Reaches out. Strokes his face.
Ash doesn't flinch.

That's good. Don't look so down. You were great.
See you.

Both him and his friend leave.

The bathroom is silent.
The stalls next to him are empty.
The area by the sinks is empty.
Ash is completely alone.

He leans his sweating forehead against the sweaty
stall wall.

Don't cry.
You heard him.

You were great.

Ash pulls his pants up and sits on the filthy toilet.
Two songs pass.

Someone raps on the door to see if it's occupied, and he ignores it. Defecators and urinators cycle through the two stalls next to him. He hears another rap on his door. A loud whisper.
–Yo, malchik. Are you in there? I've been looking for you all over. It's me.
He sings "It had to be you," undoes the latch and she pushes the door open. One look and she lurches forward with her hands outstretched and he snarls:
–Do NOT touch me!
Eu freezes in the door, awkward, helpless. He's glad that he already pulled up his pants before. There's some blood on them, but it's dark and he doesn't think she will notice. He takes two steps, falls against her, but she's strong enough to support him. He whispers:
–Devotchka. What took you so long?
The limp, wet feel of his body nauseates her.
–I looked in here earlier, but you weren't at the

sinks, so I figured you went outside, to cool off. But I didn't see you out there either. Jesus dude. What the hell happened to you?

–Nothing. But hey. I'm not a virgin anymore. And I didn't even get sick. Are you proud of me?

–Oh Ash.

She bursts into tears and it alarms him and he immediately feels bad for telling her. Should he not have? Ash gathers her into his arms, puts her head against his chest:

–Why are you crying? Shh, shhh, it's Ok. I'm fine, see? I'm fine. –He wills himself to smile, pets her hair. Every muscle of him is drained. Every molecule of him is sore.

Eu squeezes him back, too upset to even register that he's letting her.

–Ash, you are NOT fine. I'm taking you home right now!

–No way. I want to dance. I want to dance with you. You're the only person I want to see tonight. And the only person I want to dance with.

He takes her hand and leads her out on the floor.

He loses himself in the lights, spinning with her. Nobody exists but him and Eu.

9.1

He really does want to stay all night. It's just that time when the overhead lights slam on. No warning, and suddenly, it's all lardy makeup, greasy eyeliner, pores weeping chemicals, throats exhuming alcohol, tar, tonsil stones and ripening colds. The floor degrades into a discount bin of who to take home and few have stayed so late. In the harsh glare, she thinks he looks haggard; they had danced non-stop to every song in every set. He wanted to and she didn't dare refuse him. Now she's exhausted and can smell her own sweat—Eu wants sleep, but doesn't want to leave him alone.

–What are you going to do now?

She asks as they leave the club. People still hang out around the door outside, arranging rides and smoking. A mild night for late fall and not raining. They stand at the bus stop; the bus will be here in the time it takes to smoke a cigarette, which is lucky. The next one won't come until morning. Ash shrugs.

–Go home. Sleep.

His indifference disturbs her.

–Can I go with you?

–To sleep?

–To get you home and into bed safely. Someone should be with you and make sure you have enough water. But I guess your sister will keep an eye on you...

–She's not home. She spends Friday nights over at her friend's house. But won't your parents freak if you don't go home tonight?

–No. It's actually kind of a tradition that I sleep over at my friend Clara's house whenever I go to the London. They'll just think I did that. But won't your parents flip if I come over now?

–They're at work. But I doubt they'd care anyway.

The bus arrives; the driver gives them the stinkeye. Eu directs Ash to the back, where he collapses on a seat, and she next to him. It's their first chance to rest since arriving at the London the night before. Ash lays his head against her, and she shakes as each stop brings them closer to their destination.

We're going to be at his place.

Together. Alone.

All night.

Then her skin crawls for even thinking it.

They arrive and she leads him off the bus, down the street, and into his apartment. By now, Ash has slipped into a new layer of inebriation and trundles after her in a near-coma. They get in, the kitchen is its usual pit and she pushes him upstairs and into the bathroom.

–Take a shower, –Eu orders, and Ash starts to undress, not even bothering to wait for her to get out. Oh god, help me get through this. Eu dashes out of the bathroom and all but runs into his room. Picks out a T-shirt and boxers from his dresser to toss into the steam. Goes down into the kitchen. She finds an empty two-liter coke bottle and fills it with water and takes that and a glass upstairs. By then, Ash has wandered out of the bathroom, but hasn't bothered to put on any of the clothes she picked out. He's walking into his room with only a towel wrapped around his waist. Eu turns away sharply:

–Jesus, boy, put some clothes on! –And he mutters something. –They're in the bathroom!

He shuffles back, comes out dressed and stumbles into his room.

–Drink this. –Eu gives him water, but he pushes the glass away roughly. A few drops spill.

–No. I'll throw up.

–Ash, you have to drink water. Come on, –she begs.
–Just a few sips.

She thinks he'll become irate, but he obediently finishes the whole glass and then starts orbiting the room.

–Bed, –he groans, and she takes his hand, then looks at the couch under the bunk bed. It can be folded out into a full bed, which she does, and arranges the blankets. Ash falls on it and she tucks him in.

–Are you going to be alright?

–Sure.

–Ok. I left a bottle of water with the glass by the bed. I'll sit at your desk, and if you need something...

–No. Lay down, –he commands her, and she does, next to him, in all her clothes. Eu thinks her heart will burst out of her chest.

–Do you want more water?

–No.

He grips her left hand with his right one and starts squeezing it, shivering. She puts her other hand on his forehead; it's hot and clammy, and he grabs it then, using it to massage his own head.

–Your hand feels so good, –he moans, and Eu's nerves tingle.

–Ash, just go to sleep.

–No.

Everything is no. But he's already sleeping. Eu watches him, has some water herself. Her heart stopped beating so hard, it couldn't keep up that frantic pace, but she can't stop herself. Goodnight, she whispers, then leans down and gently brushes her lips against his head, barely touching him.

He says something to her then and her lungs squeeze shut.

–What? –She whispers into his ear.

He turns, his eyes still closed; he's truly asleep, she's sure of it. But still, he sighs it clearly:

Don't.

10.

Pain. Inside, outside, front to back, top to bottom.

There's a hideous taste in his mouth, his head is in a vise, and when he turns his face; his eyes widen. Eu is in bed next to him. Asleep, fully dressed. The first second, he's happy to see her, the next second the rest of the night floods his brain. He gets up and pads to the bathroom to pee out poison and brush moss from his teeth, then drinks some of the water she left in the bottle next to the bed. He's overwhelmed with thirst. The clock says it's just after daylight.

He crawls back into bed and Eu wakes up to him moving around.

–Ash?

–Yeah?

–You're awake.

–Yeah.

–Do you need water?

–Thanks, I already had some. You should probably though... –He pours her a glass and she sits up to drink it. Ash stares across the room, directing his words somewhere towards the window. –You know, I... I wanted to say thank you for getting me home last night. And taking care of me. I'm really sorry you had to do all that.

–What are you talking about? –She puts a hand on him. Last night, he liked her rubbing him so much, now, he recoils and she pulls back immediately. –As if I would leave you alone after—

He cuts her off.

–Let's just not talk about that. It doesn't matter.

–It does matter! I'm responsible! I took you there, and... it's my fault... that happened to you!

–Listen, Eu. I want to clear this up, right here, right now. What happened last night had nothing to do with you, ok? You're not my babysitter and it was not your fault. I did what I did, I made my own choices. Do you get that?

Eu wants to hug him so badly, and clutches a pillow tight instead. She asks:

–What did you take, anyway?

–Some pill.

–Jesus Christ, you can't just *take something* someone gives you in a club! Do you have any idea how fucking dangerous that is?!

Her face reddens as the words hit; his blackens.

–I think I figured it out. –Ash's tone is subzero. –But thanks. Anyway, can we not talk about it anymore? Seriously, I don't want to talk about it ever again. I mean it.

–I'm sorry. I was just so worried...

–I heard you in the bathroom, like an hour ago. You were in there for like 30 minutes. Are you okay?

Her neck tinges red and he frowns.

–Are you sick?

Eu hesitates, looks away.

–I'm fine. My stomach gets weird sometimes when I get nervous, and this thing stressed me out.

When I get nervous. Or overeat. Or feel bad. Or feel insecure. Or...

–You don't need to be doing... that. You know? You look great.

Not great enough, apparently. But she says nothing. Ash lays down and his tone lowers with contrition.

–I don't remember too much after we got on the bus. I was totally out of it by then. I really hope I didn't do anything to embarrass you.

–No. Well, you kept rubbing me and saying it felt good.

He blushes hard.

–I guess that was the drug.

–Sure.

The drug. Eu feels horrible; because he doesn't re- member; because a crummy, selfish part of her wants to go back there. She wants him to remember that he liked her. She says, –How long can I stay before your parents come home and throw me out?

–They're already home; they probably went straight to bed. My sister will be back around one though. You might want to be out by then, so she doesn't get weirded out by us sleeping in one bed.

The alarm is set for noon. Ash immediately falls sleep, and Eu lays next to him.

Listens to him breathing, steadily.

He moves around in his sleep, but never touches her.

11.

It takes Eu some time, fishing at the London, before she
finds out what exactly happened. So it was that guy, she
thinks when she finally stitches the pieces together, making sure she has all the facts, making sure she doesn't
jump to conclusions, and then she goes to the London
one more time alone before spotting Nick with the bru-
nette friend and some other person. It's between sets and
they're talking on the floor when she approaches them.

A black T-shirt hangs off her broad shoulders—
black pants—and her big black trenchcoat that goes
down to her calves. She strides right through the pit, and
puts a hand on Nick's shoulder.

–What? –He turns around and doesn't know her.
Squints. –Wait a minute. You were... with that kid, some
weeks ago. That, what's his name.

–Man you must've raped a lot of people if you can't
even keep their names straight.

–Whoa! –Nick puts his hands up. –Listen, I don't
know who the fuck you are, but that was no rape. Trust
me. –He leers now. –Your friend wanted me bad.

The next act is about to start, the lights dim. Eu steps
right up to him, pulls a switchblade from her pocket and
presses it into Nick's side. Flicks a button. A dick length
of steel flashes against his side, the blade comes to a
stop just short of his arm. In the dark, shifting crowd,
nobody else sees it. Who the hell walks around with a
switchblade? Part of Nick wants to laugh at the drama,
he might have, if she wasn't slightly taller than him and
holding a knife. The blade cuts into his leather jacket. He
gasps, shocked that she's gone so far.

His friends stare, one steps forward, Eu says

-Do not, or I will push this whole thing into him. Come see if I won't.

Nick breathes in deep, shakes his head; his friends walk off. Eu imagines they will now look for security—if she knows the London, the lone security guy is rolling or sleeping by this time of the night. Certainly not by the front door, or looking over the floor, as he is supposed to be. She has at least one song.

Eu puts Nick's head in a half-head lock, rests her face against his skull. A casual glance sees a pretty couple, cuddling as they wait for the set to start. She smells his sweat run cold.

-It's scary, huh? -Eu whispers against his neck. -When someone has control over your body. Over whether you feel pain or not.

The blade has pierced his coat. The tip of the blade rests against his bare skin now. He tries to control his breathing but it comes out ragged.

-Listen dude or girl or whatever the fuck you are. Yeah, I gave him something, but I thought he was into it. I won't go near him again. I'm sorry—

Music starts—an aggressive wave of sound crashes over their heads. She still has the blade against his skin, her face so close he can hear the rippling of wet mouth–flesh peeling back from her dental bones. The terrifying sound of a smile.

Eu says, -You're not sorry. You're just sorry you got caught. But I think that's the best we're going to get, so... Don't forget. If I EVER hear about you pulling this kind of shit with him or anyone else—ever again—this six inches, is going into *you*. All of it.

Stepping back, she flicks the blade away—thinks Nick will try to grab her, in which case it's time to activate plan B, but he just stands there, rubbing his forearm through the busted jacket.

–This was 300 dollars, –he curses, and Eu shrugs before she turns off the floor.

–Then it was a cheap lesson. Now get fucked. And die.

12.

–I'm done drawing angels, Eu. I'm going to draw something else today.

They sit in his room, listening to a CD Eu had made the night before (Queen vs. NIN)—Eu was just trying to figure out an appropriate vanishing point for her landscape when he spoke.

She puts her hand out; he gives her a ruler and she pulls a line down her paper. Asks him: –So what did you want to draw then? You can borrow this magazine I brought over, if you want. There are a lot of good landscapes in it.

–Actually, I thought I could draw you. If you don't mind.

Her breathing stops.

–But I'd have to not move for like—

–No, you don't. Just keep drawing. I can draw you like you are now, naturally. I mean, you're not going to move around much. Just stay there and keep doing what you're doing.

Eu nods and he turns his chair to face her, pushes a curtain of hair out of his face. Clips a piece of paper onto his art board and starts to scribble. It's so hard for Eu to not watch him watching her—she forces herself to focus on the landscape. Since that first day, she's looked through his sketchbooks many times. He has a ton of them—and she's even seen his much older books. Some of the books went as far back as grade school. Many sketches of his sister. All the poses were of Lena's face—often in makeup—no depiction that was even remotely suspect, but Eu knew it was still... weird. And that he was trusting her by showing her. And that he was completely unwilling to talk about it. Still, she was certain that his sister's face was the only 'real' person he had ever drawn. The rest were always fantastical beings, but now the universe of his sketchbooks would contain not just all those other fantasy subjects, and not just his sister—but Eu. She wonders if it makes sense to subscribe any meaning to that at all.

Her mind wanders over him, over her, over the night at the London. After that night, she'd been terrified that everything would change; that their outing had demolished Ash and that their friendship too, by proxy, would be irretrievably damaged, but as far as he acted, the incident had never happened. At first she thought he was merely trying to cover up his feelings, to act tough for her, but a week later, he was already asking if they could go somewhere together again and seemed to harbor no bad feelings against the London or clubs anywhere. How he truly felt about the incident, she would never know.

As it was, almost every weekend, they'd go to some club or show.

Almost every weekend, Ash would hook up with some random beautiful boy.

Eu would (less often) hook up with someone too.

And at the end, they would find each other, and go back to his house, and talk and draw and laugh about what had transpired and compare notes, and fall asleep in his bed. Somewhere close to noon the next day, they would get up, and Eu would go home, before Ash's sister came home.

This became their tradition, what they looked forward to at the end of every week. What carried them through, week by week.

And Eu realized things were more nuanced than she had first suspected. For one, while Ash preferred boys exclusively when they went out, he wasn't oblivious to girls— And his issue with touching seemed to have shifted, too. At least in clubs, he seemed less anxious, and would even touch her when they were dancing, draw her close to him; whisper and squeeze her shoulder—if she didn't know better, it would be flirting—if anyone else acted like that with her, she would call it flirting, but he never acted like that at school or anywhere else, even when they were alone together, and Eu was confused, so so confused.

Except she wasn't.

Dude, isn't it obvious? For the first time in his life, attractive people are paying attention to him. For once, he's not just the skinny little art fag. But you're still the big clumsy dyke. I mean, let's be real. Ash has some serious face-patrol. You see the type of people he hooks up with. Come on, Eu. You're too big, too loud, too masc, but not male enough. Pretty good with makeup, but not as good as him. You can't keep up. And... he'll flirt with you and keep stringing you along so you'll keep taking him to these places, but... he's never going to see YOU.

–What's wrong?

His voice cuts the silence.

Eu looks down. Her pencil had stopped moving long ago.

She snaps out of it.

–Nothing. I just spaced off. How's it coming?

–Good. –He lays a pencil down on his desk and selects another one; thicker—he starts to make bold marks. –I'm almost done.

–Will I be allowed to see it?

–If you want to.

–Of course.

She's dying to see it, actually. Eu looks down at her own drawing; she knows now that this effort will go to the wayside. Her focus has been shattered.

Ash makes a couple more marks. Selects a squibble of white oil pastel to make some highlights and judges his drawing with a critical eye.

–I don't know. Maybe you won't like it.

It's the voice she recognizes well—the dissatisfaction of the artist as soon as the work is completed. She shakes her head.

–Come on, let me see it. You said you would.

–Sure.

Ash sits down on the couch next to her, bringing the board. Lays it on their knees and as Eu looks down, her stomach churns up.

–Sorry. –He looks embarrassed, misreading the pinch of her face. –I know I said I was done with angels, but somehow, it fit.

Eu studies the paper—she would think that if anyone ever wanted to draw her, they would minimize her features or deliberately try to make her look more delicate, more feminine, but Ash had maximized everything about her,—The drawing was a portrait, from the neck up— all of it a controlled mess of slashes and angles—drawn exactly as she is looking today—her long, big nose. Hard face. Black eyes. Bruised eyes. Cragged cheeks. Graphite blood gently spatters the face. She bleeds, yet stares defiant, with the hard, blank stare of an icon The figure suggests power, even violence—yet something about it is also vulnerable.

Thirty seconds slip by.

– Damn. I don't even know what to say. I've never seen you do a portrait before.

Except of... She doesn't say it.

He's lowered his voice, for some reason, they are both whispering.

–I don't usually. It's hard to draw faces.

–Dude, you knocked this out in like... fifteen minutes.

–I don't mean 'difficult,' like... skill-wise. But you stare at the person. You look at every part of their face, their proportions, down to the details of their eyelids and the shape their hairline makes. The shape of their nostrils. The philtrum.

–The philwhat?

He touches the groove above his own lip.

– ...Then the scars, and moles and shadows on their face. The eyes. The shine on their nose and eyes. The little pink corner in the eye. The gleam on the lower lashes. You wonder if anyone's ever looked at them that closely before. It's just so...

The word he's looking for is 'intimate.'

He doesn't use that word.

–It's just really ...personal. I couldn't do a portrait for most people. And I don't like using photos. So I hardly ever draw them.

–Well then, I feel double honored. It's really beautiful. –She turns away, shyly.

–Of course. I mean, you were the model.

He's never going to see YOU.

Under the board, his knee grazes hers accidentally. He pulls it away, apologizing, and she shivers with a sudden and almost irrepressible urge.

To ask him to lean back.

To ask him to close his eyes.

To slowly run her fingers over the contours of his face.

To tangibly feel his perfection.

To memorize it with her body.

To touch him.

She breathes in sharply—Ash is staring at her and she's certain that he feels it too. The air crackles.

But then he stands up and walks back to his desk. Picks up a pencil. He's drawing something else now.

And Eu knows somewhere that she's wrong. But she also knows somewhere, that she is right.

Come on.
We said we weren't doing this!
Stop it, Eu.
He's just a fucked–up, stupid guy.
Like any other guy.
But he's not though.
If he was, your self-esteem wouldn't be such a wreck. I mean, I was actually thinking of SHAVING the other day, like—maybe my mom is right? I mean, UGH!
I keep asking,
Why can't I just fucking let it go? I don't understand WHY.
I know he doesn't owe me anything and I just want to let it go, so why not?

But Eu knows in these matters, there is no whys.
Or why nots.
It's senseless to keep looking for whys.
What would make sense is to stop looking.

13.

–Close your eyes, –Ash says to her. –Open your mouth.
Eu obeys. Something soft touches her lips.
The faint scent of vanilla beans and rich dark chocolate.
–Now bite.

She bites, eyes still closed, and once the thick chocolatey fudge spreads over her tongue, she makes a noise so dirty, even he blushes.

–Nnnnnn... God, that is fucking *good*.

–I knew you'd like it. We have a whole pan at my house—Lena made them.

–Why is your sister making you food? She must've noticed by now that you don't eat.

–Because I know you love brownies so I told her to make some. For you. -He shrugs.

–So what, she just has to do what you say?

Her tone marinates in sarcasm.

Ash doesn't pick it up.

–Of course. I'm her older brother.

The matter of fact way he says this makes her embarrassed for Lena.

Cause being at your brother's beck and call is totally normal, right?

I think if Joe or Mark ever ordered me to make something for one of their friends, I'd tear them a new ass hole. But hey. You say 'tomahtoh.' I say 'fuck you.'

–Anyway, –he says, –I got these brownies that she made and I ripped a new CD that sounds pretty interesting... some kind of Russian industrial metal.

Eu had recently gotten them on an industrial kick... She closes her eyes; pictures the afternoon they could have, like all afternoons they have together: Sitting on his couch, drawing, listening to music, talking, laughing. Hot drinks, since the weather has gotten so cold. Now there would even be brownies. She sighs with honest regret.

–Sorry, I feel really bad, because I really really want to listen to the CD and eat more of this deliciousness... but I can't today.

Ash doesn't try to hide his disappointment.

–Nooooo... Really?

–Sorry, dude.

–Wait, this is that German test you have at the end of the week, right? Just bring your stuff and study at my place. You can take the desk, and I'll have the couch.

Nor does he have any more reservations about acting like they do not spend all their time together. That point in their relationship has long passed.

Eu puts the brownie down on a napkin. She figures she should at least give him the courtesy of not having her mouth full when she tells him, so she swallows first.

–It's not the German test, Ash. I can't come over today, because I have a date.

Ash looks flabbergasted. The look annoys Eu to death.

–What, you're surprised that sad old Eu could actually get a date?!

–What are you talking about? –He bristles. –I'm surprised, because we hang out every day, and you've never even told me that you like someone, let alone that you're dating someone.

–I'm not dating someone. –Eu corrects him, icy, and hating her own tone. –I'm going on a date.

–Well, good. Good on you.

She wants his anger to be based in jealousy, but suspects it's actually in confusion. Or feeling betrayed at her not trusting him. He's right, she thinks, I've told him nothing. But what was there to say? Her friend Andrea from another school had set her up.

–Eulie, –practical Andi had said. –You have to get over this Asher dude. If he wanted to go out with you, he would have by now. So get someone new to forget about him. You know my cousin, you met at my house once, Trent, he told me he's interested in you.

–No, the last thing I want to do is go after ANOTH-ER guy. Isn't there anyone else?

–But another guy will make you forget THIS guy! He likes the same kind of music and he thinks you're hot—you could hang out downtown or something.

–We're just getting coffee, she says now, turning to Ash and he looks at her funny.

–Ok? Do whatever you want. You don't have to explain yourself to me. I was just surprised, because you never talk about anyone that way to me.

Pop quiz! Please circle the correct answer.
Are you:
A, clueless
B, a dummass
C, a nincompoop, or
D, All of the above?

Eu's putting her money on 'D'.
The words tumble out before she can filter:
–I did tell you once, and fat good that did me.
It clicks and he reddens. Oh my god, don't tell me my torch for you isn't fucking obvious?
–You're still thinking about that conversation? –He mumbles. –But I thought I was clear.

–No, to be perfectly honest, you weren't clear. Not exactly. I mean, you told me you like someone, and yes, it was a guy, but it's not like you're only into dick, right?

Ash is grateful for once that he's a loner who only has one friend. There is nobody else at their table to stare at them. Still, he lowers his voice.

–Can you keep it down? I'd like to get beat up less, not more. And no, I'm not only into... guys... or *that*... So what's your point?

–My point, Ash, is that I want to know why not me, ok? I know it's petty, but I want to know.

He fidgets now.

–Does there have to be some big reason? You're just not my type.

–Like how? Physically? Personality-wise?

–I don't know how.

–Then who is your type, for girls?

–Eu, stop it!

–No, who then? Tell me. Just give me one person from school. Anyone.

–I don't know who. I mean, you know... maybe someone like my sister, or—

Ash bites his tongue.

They both look horrified and Eu knows it's too easy, but she figures, if he's going to leave himself this wide open, the gloves come off.

–Oh my god, you narcissistic FREAK! Jesus, that's just whacked!

–W-well, of course I meant, if she wasn't my sister! Just someone like her!

He counter-sputters, but Eu plows on:

–So let me get this straight. Your ideal girl is some beautiful, bouncy, swishy-haired carbon-copy-of-yourself *babe* who cooks for you at the slightest snap of your fingers? Ugh, can you be any more misogynistic?

–…Reminding you here that English is my second language…

–Goddamn it, Ash, I mean, could you be any MORE of a sexist pig!?

–Oh I'm sorry, I didn't know being attracted to a pretty girl who's nice to me was so sexist and awful?? I think it's pretty *normal*.

–Well, I'm sorry I'm not pretty and nice enough for your normal fucking sexist standards!

–I never asked you to be! –He hisses. –And I don't know why the hell we are having this fight anyway. You're my best friend, or at least, I thought you were. We hang out so much and I see you and talk to you so much more than anyone else, even my sister, so what is the problem? Or what, that we're not physical? That our thing isn't sexual? You want me to be all over you?

–Ash, come on. You know that's not it.

But it kills her.

It's not.

But it is.

But it's NOT.

But it also… is.

Ash sees right through.

–No, I don't know that. I mean, I thought I did, but I don't anymore. You said I wasn't clear before, so then let me be crystal clear now: You will not be my girlfriend. I will not be your boyfriend. We are not going to go out.

We are not going to fuck. Ever. Got it? So if you're waiting for one of those to happen, and it's the only reason
you're keeping me around, you can stop talking to me
altogether.

He leaves the food for her on the table, gathers his
things and leaves.

Eu closes her eyes and fantasizes about shooting
herself in the head.

14.

That afternoon, Eulalie goes on a date with Trent Fore-
man.

They see a movie with many explosions, then go to
a new coffee shop near the theater and talk over caramel
macchiatos.

Trent is taller than her, pretty, and doesn't like any
band that more than five people have heard of.

After two sentences related to art, she sees that he
doesn't know Pissarro from Camero; and that B and H
have no further significance to him than the second and
eighth letters of the alphabet, respectively.

He listens to her intently though, she can tell he
likes her a lot. The only disapproval she incurs is when
she gets up to buy herself a second raspberry scone.

–Hungry, huh? –He raises an eyebrow, only a quarter joking, and she scowls.

What a bitch, she thinks and moodily buys herself a
third scone when she finishes the second.

He doesn't notice her distraction though, seems to

think everything is peachy-keen, even kisses her in his car, after driving her home in his battle–scarred Mustang. Trent kisses her mouth, her neck, he puts his hands on her chest, through her shirt. The bandages seem to perplex him, but he says nothing.

Eu lets him, figuring it's nice to have SOMEONE who doesn't mind touching her.

Buttrock blares in the background. She stops him only when his hand starts to move under her skirt.

–STOP, –she says.

Loud and clear.

He apologizes immediately and doesn't push anything else at all.

–Thanks Eulalie, –he says, when she gets out. He always uses her whole name. –I had a really great time. We should meet again.

–Sure.

–Then I'll call you?

Eu nods, steps out on the curb, depressed. He pulls away and she is wondering how someone can sound like nothing.

14.1

That afternoon, Lena Machnik is walking home alone. She passes people as she walks, and they smile at her. Even when they don't know her well, they wave. As if they want to know her. Lena's always been the type of girl that people wanted to get to know, but most people don't get the chance. And the ones who don't, can only make assumptions. Anyone seeing her walking that day would probably assume that she's a bit pampered, and most likely, stuck up. They would assume that she lives up on the hill, and is down here to visit a friend. Or maybe walking over to catch the bus to the city. She must be passing through, because they'd assume she can't possibly belong to one of those shitty complexes beyond the high school. The girls who live there wear tube tops even in the winter under loud Moncler knockoffs and date oldyoung faced drug dealers. Lena looks rich enough to do coke, and innocent enough to have never seen a joint in her life.

If they got closer to her, or talked to her a bit, they might notice: okay. Her clothes ARE pretty shabby. Still, they'd gloss over that quickly. They'd notice her smile more: cautious, but genuine. Rarely open. But if they did catch that rare flash of jagged tooth, even that would be endearing. Oh look. She is like us. But not like us. Because they sell mouthfuls of straight smiles at any suburban orthodontist's office, but not even a billionaire could walk down the street quite like she does. Especially not a billionaire.

They would never imagine that every morning, Lena Machnik prepares food for herself in a filthy kitchen. That she saves extra for the laundromat, because they do not have a washer and dryer, and her parents wash their own clothes practically never. Lena can smell her parents one aisle over, in the grocery store. It's mortifying. So she made a pact with Ash ages ago that the two of them would always pool their money for laundry and go to the laundromat regularly together. Neither of them have many clothes, and Lena knows, it doesn't matter how pretty you are—smelling bad is social suicide.

Unfortunately for Ash, being pretty and not smelling bad hasn't been enough. It's hurt Lena over the years to see how badly her brother fared. She never understood why. Since she could remember, he was the boy by which she measured all others, yet the same people who accepted her so readily kept shouting at him to get smaller and smaller. She'd watched him fold himself up, tighter and tighter, but it was never enough and she worried that one day, he'd fold himself so small he'd just pop out of existence. Completely disappear. As good as he was at looking out for her, he didn't seem to know how to look out for himself. And Lena didn't know how to protect him back either. All she could do was love him as hard as she could—but lately, even that was a problem.

Lena knew (vaguely) what he was so scared of, and she didn't understand that either. She wasn't like him, always trapped in her own head. She knew well what could and could not be. They'd shared a room ever since they had come to the states, and every move, their parents promised them their own rooms, which never materialized (a smaller apartment was one of their big money-savers). Still, Ash took care to protect her privacy and never make her feel weird. Unlike their stepdad, who relished making everyone as uncomfortable as possible. Crude jokes flew about Riva, about Ash, and these last years, Lena could feel his eyes on her, too. *I don't want you ever alone with him here while Mom is sleeping,* Ash had said to her once, point-blank. Both still in middle school. It was the one time he verbalized what they both knew, so she was careful around her stepfather. Who now had an even newer target: Eu. What her and Ash were doing or were not doing, up in their room on the weekends. It was enough to make Lena sick to her stomach. She would've liked to tell Sam: *No, that's you. That's you, staring at her. That's YOU, staring at me, when you think I don't see you. Ash doesn't do that. He isn't LIKE that.*

Speaking of—she looks up and sees a familiar figure loping a good half a block ahead of her. Lena grips her bookbag tight to her side and trots until she reaches him. And he looks surprised that his sister doesn't have Key Club today. Or dance practice. Or a study session with one of her friends. And she's surprised that Eu isn't with him. Especially when she'd baked brownies for her. Even more surprised when he tells her, it's because she's on a date. Does he look upset by that? Lena can't quite tell. Maybe Sam was right and there is something going on between them. But she doesn't think so.

When she takes his hand, he doesn't pull away. They walk next to each other and since they're both free this afternoon and that never happens anymore, Lena asks him if he would—

Once they're back in the apartment together and dump their bags in their room, they start the hunt.

Lena's Important Box – two dollars
Ash's wallet – one twenty-five
Stepdad's jeans downstairs – crumbled fiver
Bottom of mom's purse (not her wallet. She'd notice that) – two bucks in change
Couch cushions – two quarters and 30 cents

Then Ash takes a black garbage bag and they fill it with all the empty soda bottles and beer cans, and lug it down to the 7/11 on the corner. The cashier is not happy—there's no bottle counting machine, and these kids have dragged in the biggest sack of stinky, sticky bottles. He counts the deposit with pointed disdain, hoping to shame them into never doing this again—

Refund from empty cans – six dollars

They take their money and walk 1.3 miles west on the big drag, to the movie theatre complex. In the grocery store next to it, they buy small bottles of off–brand orange soda, and a king sized bag of Skittles, and a small bag of chips. Lena puts these in her purse, then they go over to the movie theatre and buy two student tickets. First, they watch a movie with many explosions (possibly the same one Eu saw). They both drink soda and Lena eats chips. Next, they watch a foreign movie with subtitles that makes them both cry. Ash picks out the lemon and orange skittles and Lena eats the purple and red ones. Neither of them likes the green. The second movie has nobody but them in the theatre, and when they're not crying, they're talking about their favorite joint plan: Saving up enough money to buy plane tickets to visit their grandmother. They had not been back once since they moved to the states...

–Do you think she'll recognize us if we just show up one day? –Lena asks, plucking a final red Skittle from the spurned greens..

–No, –he says. Thinks a bit. –Yes. I don't know.

Lena says she doesn't remember how to get to her house anymore, but he says, he does. They'll take a taxi from the airport to — and then take the red 40, six stops. He even remembers the name of the bus stop, and she remembers the derelict house on the corner where they have to get off.

After the foreign movie, Ash asks his sister if she wants to go home, but Lena says she wants to watch one more. They sneak out of theatre three and shimmy over to theatre eight, which has just started playing a Halloween remake. Ash is teasing her; he knows that Lena will need the lights on to sleep, but he doesn't mind.

He doesn't want to go home yet either.

A pimply post–teen manager sweeping near the toilets notices the two skulking into the theatre. He's the one who ripped their tickets five hours ago, and he definitely remembers them. He knows he should walk over and kick them out.

Then again, he figures, it's not every day you get hot twin girls movie hopping.

So he turns around and keeps sweeping.

15.

Ash is looking for Eulalie next day at lunch; she didn't show up at the table where they usually sit. He finds her outside, sitting down, her back against one of the sycamores, picking a big hole bigger on her black–jeans. She's wearing her depro hoodie, an XXXXXL black sweater with a satanic band on the back. A sweater big enough to swim in and swallow all her curves. The depro hoodie only comes out when something especially bad has happened and he wonders if this means her afternoon the day before had been a flop. He clears his throat.

–So, how was your date?

She looks up.

–Oh. So I guess 'talking to Eu again' was not on that long list of shit that's never ever going to happen. Whoooo. Lucky me.

I guess she's wearing the hoodie because of me.

He stares at the ground and mumbles:

–Eu, I'm sorry about going off like that yesterday. It's just that I was really looking forward to hanging out with you and listening to the new CD, is all. But we can do that anytime, so it was stupid. I don't know why I was being such a dick.

It feels good to hear him say that, but Eu thinks she may never get that corrosive tone out of her head. I will not be... You will not be... We will never...

Just don't think about it anymore.

So she doesn't.

–Anyway, –he continues. –I brought you something.

Reaching into his jacket's pocket, he pulls the item up just enough for her to see the top—

–Dude, did you steal those from your dad's dresser?

–I did actually. There's only a couple left, so I'm hoping he won't remember them. It's a nice day and not supposed to rain, so I was thinking if you feel like it, we can go over to the old cemetery after school and draw outside. You can smoke them there.

Not too long ago, Eu had shown Ash an old pet

cemetery a short bus ride away. A sort of neighborhood curiosity. Most of the tiny graves had been erected last century, and though it was fairly nicely kept, nobody ever went there anymore. They had lately taken to bringing their sketchbooks to draw under the pine trees when it wasn't raining, and Eu is feeling happy that he has asked her, but tries not to show it too much.

–Sure, –she mumbles. –We can do that, if you want. Ash, sit.

He does, covertly passes her the box, and her own jacket pocket swallows it. She says:

–Got any food? I ate my lunch already, but I'm still fucking starving.

–Ok, but are you going to... You know?

–No! I really am hungry!

–All right. I saved these for you...

He pulls out two sandwiches, flashes her the filling side and she whoops. Salami. Eu rips the saran wrap off the first one and tears into it.

–Ughhhh this is soo good. Do you ever wonder if something is weird with your mouth, because food just tastes soooo weirdly good? Wait never mind, you're the guy who hates eating. Scratch that. Anyway, about that other thing, apology accepted. –She talks while gobbling, blowing bits of bread in front of her like a woodchipper. Miraculously, he's not disgusted. –But I was the one who started being a mega–bitch, not you. So I'm the one who should apologize. I'm sorry, dude...Did I mention these are so good?

–Yeah, my mom usually splurges to get the good salami. It's the only thing she'll bother to spend money on.

–Eastern European roots I guess.

–Yeah. But hey. You still haven't told me about your date. –He grins. –Anything happen?

–We saw a shitty movie, got coffee, then made out in his car.

–Get anywhere good?

–Just second base.

–How do you order your bases?

–The regular way. So two is heavy petting.

–Really heavy?

A groan. –Normal heavy, pervert. Want me to draw you a diagram? Where he was, where I was, how he kissed, everything? Basically it was just kissing anyway. And he was good.

She feels ashamed for adding that last part, because Trent was, at best, ok.

Ash arches a brow.

–Nice. So you're going to see him again?

–Sure.

He unwraps her second sandwich while she finishes the first one, and holds it out to her, waiting patiently. She finds the gesture vaguely sweet.

–And is it love?

–I don't know, –she says breezily. –Not yet, but it could be. Looks wise, it definitely is. Taller than me. Longish, wavy black hair. ...Nice teeth.

Eu actually likes Ash's smile, but right now, she likes denting his vanity even more. Next to her, he purses his mouth tighter.

–Sounds good. So what's his name?

–Trent.

Ash frowns and she asks:

–What's wrong with 'Trent'?

–Nothing. That's just such a bullshit rocker name.

Aha, so even you're not immune to a little jealousy, huh?

He turns away sharply and some untapped sadistic streak makes her twist it.

–Well, I guess he had a name well–suited to him. He had this good rocker vibe—you know, there's just something to be said for a guy who's a real boy. The kind of guy you have to turn your face up to, to kiss. Someone who could protect you in a fight.

Ash's body stiffens next to her. He takes a sip from his orange soda.

–Well, it sounds like your date went good for you. I'm glad.

–Whatever, pal.

–I mean it, Eu. I'm not just saying that. I want you to be with someone who makes you happy.

Someone who makes me... happy.

She puts the sandwich down, dizzy.

–Ash.

–Yeah?

–I'm changing the topic. Like, really changing it. So are you ready? ...What do you know about Kandinsky?

He doesn't know why her look is so intense, and picks at the concrete under his thighs.

–Not so much but... He founded the blue rider school. He could supposedly hear color. He was part of the Russian impressionist movement. His stuff is beautiful. Why? Do you like him too? ...I was meaning to ask you anyway, if you wanted to go see the Paul Klee exhibition with me that's coming near the beginning of summer. I mean, I know it's not exactly Kandinsky, but close enough, and...

She stares at him, desolate.

Ash bites off his sentence.

–Is everything... ok?

–Yeah. I think I just consumed too many nitrates, too fast.

He stretches out his legs.

–Why don't you lay down then? We have ten more minutes until lunch is over.

He arranges his coat over his thighs and she lays her head in his lap. Eu looks up at him and then closes her eyes. You'll never grope me in a car, and you're shorter than me, and a five year old girl could kick your scrawny ass and

Who am I kidding?

Ash, it's not about the sex.

But sitting next to you and liking Kandinsky together turns me on more than the sex I could be having with someone else.

Waiting for the bell to ring with him, Eulalie hears color.

16.

Another night, getting dressed to go to the Virtue. Ash meets Eu at her house; for the first time, he sees her family and where she lives. It's a modest, well–kept split level ranch house in a nicer neighborhood on a hill above their school. Eu's family is not at all what he expected:

He had pictured a clan of eccentrics, but the strangest thing he encounters while over is her mother's zebra room. She is an avid zebra fan and has a whole room dedicated to her collection. Other than that, Eu's family is a regular group of Masons who crowd the dinner table and pass each other the tuna-fish casserole and ranch dressing. Ash pushes food on his plate, until they go into Eu's room to dress—even that is a shock. He figures Eu lore would take a grave hit if anyone from school ever saw the dessert-inspired decor. She tells him it hasn't changed since she was seven...

The most risqué item he finds is a switchblade on her desk—but then he's heard rumors that she carried one sometimes. He himself had never seen it before.

–What do you use this for? –He asks, jumping back when he presses the button and the blade flicks out.

She takes it from him, as if he were a toddler and flicks it back, then puts it in a drawer.

–Threatening people. What do you think?

Then pulls him over to her vanity dresser.

–Let me do your makeup tonight. I'll make you so pretty.

–Sure. –He says, and she keeps it light—just eyeliner with a super sharp wing, white nail-polish, then busts out her collection of leather. Eu has enough cuffs, chains, collars, and jewelry to open her own store. She picks out Ash's clothes herself—vampire-red vinyl pants and her skin-tight long-sleeve Remy-Zero shirt. Being close to the same height, they have recently taken to swapping clothes. Once their outfits are settled, Eu goes into the bathroom to change, while he changes in her room.

When she comes out, he's stiffening his hair with wax;
she puts glitter all over his cheekbones, then finishes her
own look off with two candy necklaces, fake eyelashes
and a mouth painted bright orange.

–'Mothers, lock up your sons!'... How do I look, dahling?

She pouts at him and he beckons to her.

–Mahvelous! Come here...

She leans in and he gnaws one of the candies off of
her necklace. The feel of his mouth brushing her neck
makers her close her eyes, and for that second, she lets
herself enjoy it—then pushes him off, laughing roughly.

–Those aren't for you! They're for the children!

Eu puts on insane platform boots that rocket her almost a full head taller than him; Ash pulls on his regular
boots and they walk into the hallway.

–Hey Eu, Halloween's over, –her little sister yells
from across the hall, and then stares at Ash with something approaching wonder.

–Bugger off, Katherine, –Eu yells back good–na-
turedly. –It's Halloween every day of the year.

In the living room, her mother hovers over them
while they wait for Eu's friend to come pick them up in
her car.

–I just don't understand why you always have to
wear so much make-up. You have beautiful features, you
don't need it. And orange lipstick?!

–It's a fashion statement, mom.

–Stating *what?*

–You know. –Eu winks at Ash. –*Stuff.*

–Ach, you could be so pretty if you tried.

–Except that I don't WANT to try.

–Yes honey, I can SEE that! Where did you get that dress, anyway?

–From Clara. She gained some weight and says it's no good for her anymore.

–But you think it's good for you? That plastic or rubber or whatever is hugging every roll.

–MOM, stop!

Outside, their ride blares the horn. Eu blows her mother a kiss from the door.

–Don't wait up for me, by the way. I'm spending the night at Clara's when we're done.

A big wet shameless lie: she will spend the night at Ash's, as usual, but Eu figures her mother wouldn't be thrilled to know she's sleeping alone with a boy every weekend—even if he is 83% on the boy side of bi.

–Alright, just make sure you're home by two tomorrow. Katherine has her recital. And I'll be expecting you to dress up nicely for that. Which means NO BLACK, NO SKINTIGHT, and maybe even something with FLOWERS on it?

Eu rolls her eyes more; her mother turns towards Ash, and stretches out her hands.

He just dodges a hug, pretending to have to tie his boots.

–It was so nice to finally meet you, Asher. Eulalie's told me a lot about you— you know, we do a lovely dinner over at my sister Mitra's every year for Passover and you are more than welcome to join, if that's something you'd like. Eulalie mentioned your family doesn't do anything for the holidays...

–I haven't been to a Seder dinner since I was little. I don't want to be any trouble though...

–Oh nonsense, no trouble at all! It's the least I can do, after you put up with Eulalie at your house all the time! I swear I tried to be a good mother to her—I don't know what I did wrong!

She winks conspiratorially and he smiles.

–It's no problem. Thank you for dinner, Mrs. Mason.

–Oh, but you hardly ate! That's probably why you're so nice and thin...

She giggles, a little too loudly—Eu drags him out of the house, down the lit path through their manicured lawn, growling.

–She never lost the weight after she gave birth to my baby sister, and she's still mad about it. God forbid, we don't all look like twigs. No wonder she was acting like that.

–Acting like what?

–Come on, Ash. She was FLIRTING with you.

Ash frowns.

–...She was not. She was just being nice.

They get into the car waiting for them, and it rips away from the curb.

17.

The Virtue is not like the London Theatre in many ways. It's what Eulalie would call a "real club," or maybe a real nice club, because they have actual sofas and tables and alcoves to sit—and the dance area isn't a mash of dropped butts and stomped drinks. The kids who come here are all richer twentysomethings blowing their parents' money, or lucky high school kids with an in. Eu's oldest brother spins here when he's in town and she knows the owner, so they can come for free, but they won't be served alcohol at the bar; not in such a tight-run place.

The music tonight is electronic, the theme is fetish, and the kids are crawling all over the floor by the time they get in. Eu's dress is made out of something between latex and leather, molded to her tall body, making her feel taut and hard—for once, it doesn't feel like Ash is eclipsing her— She feels all eyes on her when she strides onto the floor. Ash follows close behind, they chuck their things behind the DJ's counter and start to dance, but then Eulalie pulls him to a dark corner.

–Am I the only one who needs a little something to loosen me up?

–I thought you said they won't serve us anything here...

–Live and learn, kid. –She rogue–smiles and pulls out a flask from the top of her dress. Uncorks, takes a swig and makes a face. –Man, Wild Turkey. That is nasty.

–Then why are you drinking it?

–To get drunk, of course. No, the real reason is to be a slightly better dancer.

Ash takes a swig too, a couple more with her, and then they move out to the floor again.

–Damn, they let out the fine-looking boys tonight, –she whispers to him.

Sexy Danish house pulses through the air. Loud enough to penetrate their skin, their brain, their flesh. Ash feels the music open his veins, so does the alcohol and he starts to move. His hands go down on Eulalie's waist; she laughs, dusts a kiss on his cheek, he lets her, here, when they dance, he always lets her, then she wipes off the big orange mark with a finger. It feels good, where her mouth touched him; hot from the booze.

–Some fine girls too, –he whispers back, looking at Eu.

–Oh, are we aiming for a girl tonight, dahling?

Ash vagues out.

–I don't know. We'll see, right?

He leans close to her ear then.

–What about you and handsome Trent? Are you putting him on the side today?

–Like you said, we'll see, right?

They dance, until Eu sees a someone at the bar; their clothes fall all the right ways—

–Speaking of girls, I think my birdie just landed. Check it. 12 o'clock.

He looks, approves. She pulls him back, joking.

–I saw her first! Catch you later.

Eu, hang on. Let's dance. Just a couple songs. One song.

The words lodge in his throat.

She walks right up and Ash watches her make the approach—he's not used to seeing Eu so confident, and he wonders how much Wild Turkey she really had. The girl turns when she taps her on the shoulder and they start to talk. Half a cigarette in, the girl motions for Eu to sit on a stool next to her. Eu won't be coming back any time soon. Sad that she's gone, Ash turns away from the bar so he can't see them anymore. The floor is getting more crowded and one song later, he accidentally elbows someone hard. Watch it, they growl before he has a chance to apologize. Feeling in a dark mood himself, Ash turns to retort. And bites his tongue. A raver kid glowers up at him, he cannot be taller than 5'5, but with a mess of shaggy tawny hair, framing a serenely beautiful face. Made even prettier by scorn. Ash's organs shiver, he straightens his back. I'm sorry, he murmurs and he can tell with satisfaction that the guy is already regretting being rude to him.

17.1

56 minutes later, Eu is making out with Micah.

They stand in one of the catacomby hallways leading off of the dance floor.

Strangers brush by them on their way to the bathroom, to fix their face or do a bump. Eu pays them no mind.

Micah is wide-shouldered. Curvy. Black-eyed. Pierced. Plays the bass.

Unlike Trent though, she's not a moody snoot.

And unlike Ash, she's not fucking elusive.

On the contrary, she's quite direct. Thank god, as Eu herself would have been too shy. Micah says:

–I can't believe you're Joe's little sister. He'd KILL me.

–I won't tell him if you won't.

–I have to say, did not recognize you under all that PVC, Eulie.

Yeah, it's been a while. I've grown seven inches, lost the braces, gained forty pounds. Learned how to use foundation. Sort of.

Once they started talking, it took Eu only a moment to realize this was the same girl who used to come play in their garage, back when Eu was an all elbows metal-mouth preteen, creeping around the peripheries of the garage. Joe would shoo her away—

–I said, scram!

Sometimes, he'd even throw things at her, just hard enough to show he wasn't joking, and once, Micah intervened:

–I don't mind if your little brother sticks around.

–Mikey, that's my little sister.

–Whoops. Sorry.

–And don't encourage her. Or she'll sit here and *eye-hump* you all afternoon.

Thankfully, Micah either doesn't remember those details or isn't bringing that up—

Eu bites her lip while the girl runs her hands down over her latexed body and she laments choosing this particular dress to their outing tonight. It's impossible to maneuver in any kind of discreet way.

–I should've worn something else, –she grumbles and Micah shakes her head vigorously.

–But this outfit makes me wanna peel you like a Babybel cheese.

God, Eu thinks, this girl smells so good. I just want

to go home with her, split a blunt with her, have her skin me out of this dress and then... And then WHAT? Jesus Christ, Eu, she's 24! Are you crazy? That's even older than Joe!

Yeah, just means she'll actually know what the fuck's she's doing for a change and not be absolute shit at sex. If she asks, you better go with her—

And what, leave Ash here?

Yeah, why not? You think he wouldn't leave you?

No, he would not.

Oh my fuck, can you not moon over that little twat for five minutes? Stop being a clown and if she asks, GO WITH HER.

Micah sucks her neck, then pulls back, looks her right in the face.

–Want to get out of here? I live just around the corner and I've got some good weed.

Eu wants to holler. Hallefuckingluia. Earlier, she'd been casually asked, so how old are you now? and Eu'd breezed that she's 20. With the height and makeup, it wasn't a stretch, and now this girl actually wanted to take her home and smoke her out, after she's been kissing her up against a wall for the last thirty minutes, kissing her fifty thousand times better than Trent could ever hope to kiss, and she already told her mom she's going to Clara's afterwards and has a clear alibi, and Ash is undoubtedly grinding up on some dude in some corner and hasn't thought of her once in this last hour, so just go with her, just go with her... just.

Eu says:

–I would love to, but I came with someone else.

Micah raises her eyebrows.

–You mean, the nimrod who's let you out of their sight for an hour now?

–We just came as friends, but I would still feel bad, leaving without saying anything. Anyway, I left him first—because I saw you.

This seems to mollify her.

Micah puts another kiss on her neck, then takes Eu's hand to lead her back to the main room.

–Then find them and tell them that you're going. If you want to, that is. You don't have to.

–...I want to. I do.

Eu bites her lip again, nods, they are back in the big space. Everything swims in a purple milky color. Trentmoeller vibrates through her bones.

Part of her is already steeped in regret; she shouldn't have said anything before and just left when offered back in the hall. Now she has to strain her eyes in the pulsing dark, trying to decode every couple she sees on the floor. It feels voyeuristic and sad and dismantling of her resolve. Micah says she will help, what does your friend look like?

–He's kinda tall, really skinny and...

–...And?

–Vulnerable looking.

–OK. There's a tall skinny dude looking forlorn by the second couch. That him? Next to the two hot girls making out... Ooof.

Micah extends an arm. Eu follows the line her arm makes—

She hardly even sees who she is actually pointing to though, because her eyes are drawn immediately to a splash of red, the 'girls' two feet over. It's Ash—long back straight up on the ornate couch, knees pressed together, sitting like some teen emperor with a seraphic boy perched on his lap.

Kissing him like it was the last thing he would do on this earth.

She watches them, consumed.

–And? –Micah asks. –Is sad-boy him?

Eu shakes her head, extends her own arm, and points squarely to the couple. After a beat, she says 'red pants.'

Micah nods.

She observes Ash for a few seconds; then she turns to observe Eu observing him, and then all she says is, oh. A few more moments pass, Micah suddenly hugs Eu to her tightly. Her arms are soft and strong and they say to Eu that she knows exactly what is going on, and that it will be OK, but Eulalie is not so sure.

The pit of her stomach tells her that it might just have reached the furthest point from 'OK' yet.

18.

The night is almost over.

After Micah left, Eu danced with a few others, but nobody grabbed her fancy long enough. At best, they gave a few moments of romantic escapism. She looks around; it's almost two now. She'll have to find Ash and pry him off of whoever he's with, because they need to catch the last bus home. The stop is a clippy ten minute walk from here, and if they miss it, there will be no more buses until the morning. Despite the evening's ups and downs, she figures now they'll be alone and have the chance to relax. She's looking forward to it.

–Hey Eu.

The sound of his voice makes her turns around. Ash looks sober, thank god, but his arm is still wrapped around that sweet–looking kid's shoulder—she wonders if they've been kissing all night. From the looks of it, she'd say yes: Ash appears dizzy and flushed, and his tone is a little edgy. Probably from sexual frustration.

–This is Jon.

Eu shakes the guy's hand—he seems like a fine enough sort, but she wants to get going. Come on, swap spit or phone numbers or whatever you need to do and let's go. But Ash jams his hands behind his back and won't look at her.

–So, Jon came here by car... He said he would give us a ride home. We don't have to run to make the bus.

The way he unveils this information makes Eu very suspicious: His tone is colored with the impatient whee-dling of kids trying to pull one over their parents.

–Is he even old enough to drive?!

A scowl.

–He's seventeen.

–And does Angel-Face live in our neighborhood, or what? Aren't we totally out of his way?

Ash looks at her emphatically.

–No, because he's going home. With us.

Eu stifles a pterodactyl scream.

No, he's going home with YOU. Not us!

Her glare is lethal.

Jon pretends to need the bathroom and tactfully gets lost for the next few minutes.

–Devotchka, what's up?

Ash's hands rub on Eu's shoulders; he's actually touching her when they're not dancing and her mood plummets further. You manipulative little boy b i t c h. No, don't look at me, stop flirting with me to get what you want.

She's incredibly annoyed, because she can feel it *working*.

Her tone is already softened.

–Well, I didn't bring my house key, because I thought I didn't need it, you know? So how am I going to get into my house?

–Just come to my house, like we planned?

–Ash, no offense, but I am not sleeping anywhere in your place if it's not your room. I don't dare.

He flushes a violent red and she thinks, to hell with tiptoeing.

–And I'm not going to take your sister's bunk while you're... you know. Entertaining someone below. Just drop me off at Clara's. I'll knock on her window and she'll let me in.

–No, I told you you could come over tonight and I came with you. I'll just tell Jon it won't work.

He looks miserable.

–Come on, stop the long face. Far be it from me to deny your bed a raver beauty. Why can't you just drop me off at Clara's?

–Because I feel like an asshole, kicking you out of my house, when I invited you to come over.

–Oh but forcing me to listen to you shag your uber-cute little boyfriend all night does NOT make you feel like an asshole? –She fumes.

–You won't hear anything. I'm *quiet*.

–Yo malchik, I really fucking didn't need to know that!

Jon is back—the issue is not resolved. Eu simply walks out to the street. They find his car and she directs him to her friend's house, sneaks through the garden then raps and raps on Clara's basement–room window— nobody comes to answer. The neighbor's dog starts to howl. Across the street, a light turns on in a window. Eu is afraid of potentially waking someone else in the house and creeps back to the car.

–I guess I'll be coming with you guys after all.

High, chill, or zen, Jon seems completely indifferent to all new additions to the plan. He drives them over to Ash's apartment, while Ash briefly explains the situation regarding his parents and the mess downstairs, but Eu doubts he cares one way or the other. They park outside of the complex and walk in; it's freezing and the two boys walk ahead. They're already kissing in the doorway when Eulalie and her aching feet catch up to them. Get a fucking ROOM, you two. Oop wait, that's what we're here for. Ash unlocks the door and quickly leads Jon upstairs, to avoid exposing him to the smell—he throws a final glance at Eu over his shoulder before he gets out of sight; a furtive, desperate look that says, please, don't hate me.

It doesn't work.

She hates him.

Burn in Hell.

Burn in Hell.

Burn in Hell.

Upstairs, a one hour shower starts—god, she thinks, can you even WASTE enough water? She locks out the sound by turning on the TV, loud, and then turns on all the lights downstairs. Extreme chaos makes anything but full lighting sinister. She sits on the stained couch for a couple commercials, then looks around. Clothes everywhere. Most of them, she realizes, are clean—unfolded laundry. Dirty dishes—on the floor, piled on the coffee table. Cans, bottles littering everything. In her boredom, she goes into the kitchen and finds some garbage bags and starts to pick up the bottles and trash. She folds the laundry.

Upstairs, the water finally stops running.

She runs the sink full of hot soapy water and scraps the plates into the trash and starts to soak them.

Ash and Jon move into his bedroom.

She turns the TVs volume up one tick further; the cat saunters down from upstairs. Over the months, it's gotten used to Eulalie and has even gotten to like her. A tad. The cat threads between her long, platformed legs, while she washes the dishes. They don't have a dishwasher, and she dries the dishes with some tea towels she finds folded up in one of the drawers. She puts the dried plates away, drains the sludgy water, fills the sink with hot, clean water.

Takes out the garbage, cleans up the cat litter, sorts the bottles and cans, and moves the folded laundry into empty baskets. She's sad that it's so late—it means she won't be able to find the vacuum and completely finish the job. It would be too noisy. But looking around the bottom floor of Ash's apartment that late, late night, or early, early morning, she sees it clean for the first time.

When she sits on the couch, the cat jumps on her lap, hunkers on her thighs, and catches a claw on her tights.

–I did a pretty good job, huh, Morris?

She doesn't know his actual name. All cats to her are Morris. Morris purrs his ascent, she scratches between his ears and lets out a deep sigh.

It's Saturday morning. I'm dressed to kill. And I'm sitting downstairs in Ash's apartment, that I've cleaned. Alone. I've got nobody, but Morris. Whose name isn't really Morris. Man, is this an A-list pity party, or what?

Someone on TV implores her to buy a cream that will make her silver look brand-new, so that she'll never be embarrassed by her tarnished flatware again.

Upstairs, Ash moans so loud, that she can hear it all the way downstairs.

So much for being quiet, she thinks, and that's when she starts to cry.

19.

Eu wipes something sticky and rank from her face.

It's drool.

Her head lolls uncomfortably to one side, but the couch was too short for her to stretch out on, so she slept upright. Now she jerks her head up, rubbing webby moisture from the corners of her mouth, embarrassed. Ash looks down at her. He's wearing boxer briefs and nothing else. His neck is plastered with hickeys and the glitter has migrated from his cheeks all over his body.

The expression on his face is some strange cocktail of drugged contentment and deep repentance.

Eu looks up at him.

You kidding me, fucking hickeys?

Don't be mean.

–Looks like you had a good night.

–No... I...

He tries to play it down, but she can tell he's elated.

–Ash, I'm... I'm glad you had a good time. –She's surprised and he seems surprised too, at her sincerity, and achingly grateful.

–I'm so sorry you had to spend the night down here alone. I...–He blushes furiously. –I cleaned up, so you can come sleep upstairs now. Wow, you really cleaned up. My parents won't even believe it.

–Tell them it was the kids with the wrenches. They're always up to no good.

–Sure, –he mumbles. –The kids with the wrenches. Thank you, though. It looks really great.

–I had nothing better to do.

–What happened to that cute girl you were talking to at the beginning of the night? I was sure you were going to go home with her.

Eu shrugs, Gets up. She's not in the mood for club-rehash chitchat.

–I'm going to walk home. See you Monday.

–Eu, it's six in the morning. Your parents will think some thing's wrong, if you show up now.

Something is wrong.

–I need some air.

He looks desperate.

–Then I'll open the window. You really should sleep though. Why don't you come upstairs?

Maybe because I don't even want to be in the same SOLAR SYSTEM as you right now, let alone the same room!

–Maybe Ash, –she growls, –because I don't want to sleep in a room that reeks like gross boy sex.

His torso stiffens, they stare at each other for the duration it takes his entire upper body to redden. Ash mumbles at a point somewhere outside the living room window.

–I opened the windows, and it... d-doesn't smell like anything, so will you please just come upstairs and get some rest? My parents will be home soon...

After everything else, she has no more fight left. Eu shrugs, starts to go upstairs and he follows her into his room. The couch is turned down into the futon—there are different sheets from normal. A different blanket. It is the only evidence that the dream of Jon was real. Slut. Slut. Slut. Slut. Slut. Slut. Slut. Slut. Slut. She wants to make a final crack about Ash's conquest, but just sits down on the bed. He helps take off her elaborate platforms and peel her out of her dress, gives her a T-shirt and boxers to change into. When she gets back from the bathroom, he's setting the alarm.

She lies down and he doesn't know what to say, so after 'goodnight,' he starts to walk out. But Eu sits up.

–Ash.

–Yeah?

–Just get into bed.

–I thought... that you're really mad at me.

–Goddamn it, I AM, but it's your bed, and it's big enough, and it's not like I'm going to ...*try anything*, so why the hell would you sleep down on that dirty, crusty couch that's too short for you anyway?!

He nods, cowed by her anger that he knows is partially deserved, then crawls into bed next to her and stretches out on his back.

Turns off the light.

Her eyes are closed, but she can feel his body next to hers, how it sinks into the mattress. The heat of it.

She thinks of Jon.

She imagines them for the briefest moment, kissing in the hot shower.

Meine Gott, hilfe mir dieses Toedliches Leibe zu ueberleben.

Lord God, help me survive this deadly love.

Eu lies on her back, a foot from Ash's passed out body.

He's already in a deep sleep.

She listens to his rhythm, his breathing, her fingers grip the sheets around her, to stop herself from running a hand over his arm. The moments when she'd really hated him, she'd told herself, he was a freak, a creep—how was she any better? She'd touch him now, wouldn't she? If she knew he wouldn't wake up from it. If she knew she could get away with it. No, it wasn't that.

Ash. You don't have to get into the shower with me. Or kiss me.

But can't you ever just...

If he even once reached over, and grabbed to squeeze her hand, it would be enough.

A leftover tear rolls down her face.

Her eyes stick on the ceiling.

God, fuck everything.

20.

They stand in a shower of hugging girls, staring at the cast list.

The cast list is another instrument teaching Eulalie Mason that life is not fair.

Orestaia: Part 3 Eumenides
Cast List Drama Club
Please be prepared to do a full read–through on Thursday@3:30 pm – Fulmann Auditorium. Pick up your scripts first from Jacob!!!!

Orestes: Asher Machnik
Ghost of Clytemnestra: Nicci Dramagirl
Athena: Fiona Popular
Apollo: Max Dramaboy
Fury 1: Madi Dramagirl
Fury 2: Emi Trackstar
Fury 3: Jasi Dramagirl
Fury 4: Landon Dramaboy
Zip:Eulalie Mason
Nada:Eulalie Mason
Jack shit: Eulalie Mason
Zero: Eulalie Mason

–Holy balls. You got the lead??!

She looks over at speechless Ash and squeezes his hand without thinking.

–Dude, that's so awesome! Congratulations!

He stiffens—because she didn't get a part too, or because she touched him. A few people throw him a congratulations, and he throws some back to them, and then him and Eu walk out of school, to go to his house.

It snowed a couple of days ago, and each winter day since then has added a fresh coat. The snow that sticks is rare in these parts, so they trudge in the white blanket happy as huskies. Eulalie picks up a handful, pats it into a ball and flings it at him. Crystals of ice explode on his back. Ash reaches down with both hands, and starts to pelt her back. They run through the streets, laughing.

–Hey Ash, my boy, you must be starving! You're skin and bones!

She jokes, right before they reach his apartment, and he takes the cue. They don't walk home yet, but over to the 7/11 on the corner of the big boulevard.

–Get whatever you want, this is your victory day. My treat, –she tells him while they cruise through the store, selecting a dizzying array of Hostess Ding-Dongs, Twinkies, single serving cups of ice cream with the little wooden spoon and then Eulalie goes to the hot–drink dispenser to concoct them each a gigantic Styrofoam cup mixing the various flavors.

Over in the tiny frozen food section, a girl with a double–pierced lip and a gloriously huge black coat stares at them. She moves away when Ash catches her eye, but continues from another vantage point when she realizes Eu hasn't seen her yet.

The checkout person (not the same counting the crusty bottles that one day) clucks at the calorically extravagant purchase, Eu pays, and they walk to sit outside on the curb— But it's too cold to sit, so they walk instead, perambulating the whole neighborhood. The conversation drifts all over.

Random people: That girl by the pizza case was totally in love with you. You should've asked for her number. At least one of us should have a girlfriend.

Relationships: So you never called Lil Angelface back? Ugh, don't even ask about Trent. I don't know what we are... I'm starting to think I don't work with girls OR guys...

Self-image: Fuck this meatshell. Sometimes, I think I just want to be a guy. Dating guys. But ass-sex?? Ouch. No thank you. And giving a blow job sounds fucking degrading...I dunno. I think it's pretty nice. Ash dude, TMI... But I guess that's how it goes huh? You have to blow if you want to get blown back?

Art: Yeah, I still have your conte crayon set. Ok, but I bought this new oil pastel. It was expensive, so I only got one, but the pigmentation is INSANE. You have to try it out when we get in. I still have your still-life up too...

Theater: Dude, you knocked that reading out of the park. I guess you're going to be playing an enraged motherkiller. Have you even hit anyone before? You can practice on me. I'll hit you first, and you hit me back, one degree harder...

They walk long enough to freeze all their fingers.
And their toes. Chilled water creeps up a third of their
pants' legs. She'd taken out her Discman. Earphones. Today, it's Queens of the Stone Age. The air at the bottom of
the sky's dome is a canary color and both of them stand
for some moments, eyes closed, mouths open, trying to
catch flakes on their tongues.

*Doesn't fresh snow on your tongue taste better than
anything?*

The sun dips quick, but they don't want to go back
to his place yet.

They are completely happy, like every afternoon.

Some part of Eu knows it though.

These days are over.

21.

People at McMillan High don't look at Asher Machnik the same anymore. The people who used to ignore
him now smile at him. The people who used to beat him
up now ignore him.

Even his one-time tormentor has made an uneasy
peace; randomly paired on a physics project, the boy that
once registered as the Taller One talks about meeting at
his house to finish the lab together. Ash could stay over
for dinner, if they end up working that long? As if he had
never ganged up on him in a dirty bathroom stall. Ash
only scowls at him.

He doesn't see Eulalie nearly as much as he used to,
but that can't be helped.

The drama club meets almost every afternoon to rehearse their play and when he isn't trying to memorize his lines or working with the cast, he's in the library, catching up on school work. The quarter is drawing to a close and he needs to pull his grades up. He's made new friends, his co–stars from the Orestaia, because enforced closeness has forced them to become close. Ash even has a girlfriend now: the tall, elfin girl who plays Athena. Fiona isn't complicated; she doesn't ask him for much. They don't have time for much either; just scorching looks across the theater at each other, or slow kissing back stage, when they are killing time during Act I.

In the beginning, he invites Eu to sit with his new friends at lunch—he hopes that she'll absorb into the group, but she opens with a Mother Theresa joke—segues effortlessly into dead babies. Worst is that her noxiousness seems deliberate and curated. Letting him know she does not want to be here. And will not try. Ash worries he will now be forced to choose between his new friends and her, but Eu makes it easy. After a few cumbersome attempts, she avoids his group at lunch—in fact, starts avoiding Ash altogether. And he's not entirely sure what to make of it.

Of course, he misses her. But not having Eu around makes it easier for him to cut his hair shorter again (the director had asked him to, for the show). To tone down the tight pants and the jelly bracelets and he wonders if Eu is writing him off as a sellout and a pleb. But if she is, she makes no indication. It's not that she seems angry or disappointed in him, as he is definitely not trying to push her away either. Simply, a chasm of circumstance has opened wide between them and Ash has no clue how to bridge the gap.

Before, they spent all their shared lunches and breaks together too, skipped classes together, but Eu's made herself scarce around him. She doesn't sit at their old table either, only wanders around alone outside during the lunch period.

Sometimes, he sees her through the window, her long, sharp figure cut out against the parking lot's concrete. Her hair whips in the cold January wind, and she stares into the distance. Often, she's listening to music on headphones. He wonders then what she's listening to. What she's thinking about. He wants to run out to her but something always stops him.

He does think about her often though.

Things remind him of Eu all the time.

And sometimes they pass in the hall. His arm winds around Fee; or the two of them kiss deep against a locker. His eyes might meet Eulalie's then across the crowd; real or imagined.

Her eyes say:

Mother, did it need to be so high?

Ash doesn't have an answer to that question.

21.1

His girlfriend rattles off all the prom gossip, like had he heard that Eric Swenson had asked his little sister out for prom? Dang, isn't it just gross when senior guys perv on underclass girls, so *predatory,* but the best part is, that Lena had REJECTED him—

Yes, apparently, there was someone else she would rather go to prom with, but that person supposedly already has a date! Fee spends four sentences trying to guess what kind of boy Ash's little sister would reject the most popular guy in school for, then she launches into a detailed description of her own potential prom dress—the place she will buy it, the color scheme—and what Ash needs to wear to match with her, and what kind of corsage he will have to buy for her to wear, and what kind of car she would like them to rent, and potential restaurants that could be nice, and whose house they will be spending the night at afterwards, her friend Lacey who lives up on the hill, in the neighborhood with all the rich kids (Eu's neighborhood too, actually, though her house is on the other side of that hill, with the more humble 70s split-levels, not the brand new community gated palaces with four bedrooms and a pool.) Lacey's parents' house has five bedrooms and a pool, and a rec room, and a built in bar, and her parents are going to be gone all weekend, but they are super chill, so Lacey is allowed to invite her friends over after prom, and her best friends will be allowed to spend the night, of which she is one, and in honor of their best-friendship, Lacey will let Fiona and Ash have their own room, because she knows they've been going out for a while now, and she knows that Fiona thinks Ash is very special, and now Fiona looks to the side, and her cheeks blush peach tones, well yes, she knows she's said she wanted to wait until marriage for THAT, (Fiona wears an expensive, small gold crucifix that dangles just two inches under her throat) but well yeah, this might be one of the only times they'll get to be alone and they could actually have their privacy for once, and maybe—well, you know...

She looks bashfully for his reaction to this, but Ash is still stuck back on the car he should rent for the night, wondering if she even knows that he doesn't have his permit, let alone his license; and there is no way his parents would be able to give him money to rent a suit and take her out to a nice dinner. But it's almost two months away. He'll find a way to break this to her somehow. And then she's already on another topic anyway. She's talking about her own mother, and how her mother wants to meet Ash, wants him to come over and have dinner with their family soon. Apparently, she got very curious about him once Fiona accidentally mentioned that he didn't go to Bible study; didn't go to their church at all. Well, was he going to? Fiona said she didn't think so; someone else at school said he might be Jewish... According to Fiona, her mother made quite a deal of this new bit of information, acting like being Jewish was weird or something but Fiona told her mother not to worry, yes, her boyfriend is Jewish, but he's not JEWISH Jewish, you know, Eastern European yes, but it's not like he wears a yarmulke, not that there's anything wrong with wearing a yarmulke—Thankfully, Fee never stops her monologue to ask him a question, because he's stopped listening over ten minutes ago. Ash fantasizes about sitting in a room with someone else.

Pink Floyd plays in the background.

They draw together and do not speak.

She's drawing.

Her Discman to her upper right.

A pack of Oreos (one row missing by now) to her upper left. In the background, her mother Yasmin circles the kitchen island, takes a loud, smacky sip of the iced coffee she got herself on the way back from grocery shopping, then walks over to the sink. Suddenly, the tumble of ice hits Eu's ears; crackling and hissing. Her mother had poured her ice coffee into the sink and is now using the rinsing nozzle to hose whipped cream down the drain.

Eu sits at the kitchen table, listening to her mother sing under her breath while she hoses slushysweet coffee away. She knows that if Yasmin is in a passable mood, she will leave the kitchen now, and go watch TV in the den (it's her weekly half day off from the music shop.) If she's not in a good mood, she might tell Eu that just like iced coffee, those Oreos are full of empty calories too. If she's in an after-school special comfort porn mood (the least likely), she might pull a chair up to the table. Say something like, it's been so long since we talked. Mark told me you're spending every afternoon here now. Where's that...? And if she's in an awful mood, she'll pick a fight; start saying that if only Eu pulled herself together; if she bought different clothes, and changed her hair, lost some weight, and painted over her spiky attitude, she wouldn't have to sit alone each day, drawing by herself and stuffing cookies into her face. To which Eu will have no choice but to slowly, insolently, slip an entire Oreo onto her tongue and tell her mother behind a mouthful of those rich, coal-colored crumbs that as long as Nabisco exists, there will never be any person whose bullshit is worth putting up with. However none of these scenarios happen. The evidence washed away, Yasmin pours herself a glass of water from the fridge, asks her daughter to keep an eye on the lasagna she's put in the oven and walks out. Eu spends the early evening alone. And she is happy about that.

Between her younger sister's genius and her older brothers' shenanigans, Eu's consistently kept a low profile on the Mason family radar, and she's never minded. Now especially so. She knows, it would be hard to explain what exactly is passing through her these days. It's a complicated feeling. She misses Ash. Of course, she does. She misses his light silence (never sticky or heavy). The little things he always brought her. Food, music, cigarettes. Like their old cat leaving birds on her coverlet. Like she is always on his mind, even when they're not together. She misses how he could make even a trip to the crappy corner store feel so special (in contrast, it is a wonder to Eu how crushingly *unspecial* Trent manages to render even unusual activities.) She misses all that, but she doesn't miss the clammy insecurity. The tears. That humiliating, nonstop *covetousness*. She doesn't miss how unexpectedly *selfish* he could be. Lately, she's been feeling it. All those corners in her consciousness filled to the brim with him, slowly receding and emptying, until those spaces could now carefully fill back up with herself. She can spend the afternoons listening to CDs he'd made for her, drawing and eating Oreos and sitting in peace—enjoy the essence and beauty of Ash, without the hurt. She can look at herself in the mirror, and tell herself, it is okay to look like this. It's not good, it's not bad. It's just how she looks. Even if he isn't attracted to it. Even if she'll never look like the people he is attracted to.

She can look down at her drawings (getting better every day) and feel happy that she is getting better. Her style is different from Ash's: a comic style. Simple. Good. She draws four-panel comics about the music scene. She's even shown a couple to Mark, ready for the big brother pact of ridicule anything I do to be activated. But Mark just said, hey, these are good! You got more? Can I have a copy of this one? Cam would find this funny as shit. Her dad agreed to let her borrow the Xerox machine in his band office to gather all her comics into a zine. It feels good to work on something. It feels good to get better.

Every day, she is getting better and...

It feels *good*.

22.

Now that, he thinks, is a hot girl.

22.1

It's an unusually warm early spring day and she sits on
the big wall outside.

A full, gauzy, dove-colored dress (uncharacteristi-
cally not black!) that comes off her shoulders, the peek
of bandages on her chest underneath, black stockings
and platform, buckled boots up to her knees. Inkblack
hair fresh shaved up the sides, the long part piled on her
head; mouth painted the color of an electrocuted straw-
berry and eyes shaded with heart-shaped sunglasses
with rims in the same color. On her left hand, plastic
bracelets go almost up to her elbow. In her right hand, a

book she's reading. She wears fauxleather gloves without fingers, phosphorescent French-tipped nails, and sucks on a cherry lollipop. Ash stops in front of her.

–Hey you.

She looks up. Closes her book.

–Do I know you, handsome?

He smiles lopsided and puts out his hand.

–My name's Ash.

–Sweet name. –She pretends to be thinking. –I think I do know you. You're the kid who played that ancient matricidal hottie, Orestes. I was the person who kept sending you roses anonymously. Now we've finally met.

–Ah, so now I know my hidden fan's identity. I had no idea she'd be this pretty.

Eu's cheeks flush.

She pulls the sucker out of her sparkling mouth.

–Lay it on thick? Anyway, wachu need?

–Nothing. ...Just wondering if you're busy.

–How come?

–I mean, if you're not, you could come over. If you want.

–Mmm, like the good old days, huh?

–Something like that.

–What's wrong, your girl's too busy to give you attention today? –She doesn't wait for his answer. –I would like to come over, but I'm going to be leaving soon.

–You're going out... with someone?

He looks at her outfit and she flounces her skirt.

–You think Eulalie Mason busts out her couture for the fashion serfs at McMillan High? No thank you. I've got a date.

–With Trent, the handsome rocker?

–You got it. A friend of his is spinning at this neato place. It's up in Vancouver though, so we're going over early. They're going to pick me up here in less than an hour.

–Ahh. ...I haven't been to a party in ages.

–Yup, yup. They're just as fun as ever.

She can tell he wants her to invite him. She doesn't. Instead, Eu actively savors the awkward silence.

Finally, he says:

–So, you're going by car?

–Yeah, Trent's driving, and it's going to be me and him and a friend of his.

–So ...there's one more spot free in the car? If I pitch in for gas?

His face turns a furious color. A slow second drips past. Eu sinks the sucker into her mouth, then grasping the wall's edge, suddenly unfurls her long leather–bound legs from under her and wraps them around Ash's knees, pulling him to her. He's too surprised to struggle. She raises one eyebrow and sighs:

–My darling. Was there some part of the word "date" that you did not understand?

Ash twitches between her legs, breaking out in a visible sweat. One thing is for certain, he cannot remember Eu being neither this seductive, nor this mean. He stammers.

–It's j-j-just that you said there was another guy going with you, so I thought it wasn't a formal date.

She unhooks her legs, nudging him away with the toe of a boot and pulls them back under her dress.

–Hmm. I guess you have a point. But won't your girlfriend get pissy with you going off in a car full of ponced-up folk?

–She doesn't have to know.

–What you do on the down-low?

Tell me, why am I so... fucking... KIND?

Eu glares at her studded watch, then flicks a neon-yellow nail at him as dismissively as a baroness.

–Fine. You have 45 minutes to go home, get *beautiful*, and get your skinny ass back here. If you're not here when Trent pulls up, you're SOL.

23.

–I guess he's not coming.

Eu sits in the backseat of Trent's car, facing out the back window. Trent sits front; friend shotgun—the two boys are pouring over the directions to the first location, but now they're ready to leave.

–Alright. Are you sure you don't want to wait a few more minutes?

Trent is considerate, the way boys are when they want to make a good impression. And looking at Eulalie in the rear mirror, he thinks that tonight, he wants to make a real good impression. They have been seeing each other on and off for four months now and still haven't had sex, not yet, but if all goes right, tonight's the night.

–I don't mind, –he says sweetly.

She puts on another coat of neon lipstick.

The fuck is Trent being all cute for? It's weirding me out. Oh wait a minute. I forgot. He wants to screw me. Well, I guess tonight's the night I let him. No reason to put it off more.

She flicks her eyes up at him in the rearview mirror.

–No, I told that little wanker to be here in 45 minutes and it is now 46 minutes. We run a tight ship. Hit the gas.

She's even bitchier than normal. Oh well, she looks good. You can make it up to me later, babe.

Trent shrugs, and he has just put the key into the ignition when Eu turns, looks out the rear mirror one last time. She sees someone coming out through the main double doors of the school:

Skintight jeans, patched and ripped all over.

Studded belt. Big boots.

School boy innocent white shirt with a starched collar. Top two buttons open.

Dog-tags. Dog-collar. Black trenchcoat down to his ankles. (It's Eu's old coat he borrowed months ago, and had yet to give back.)

His hair (it's gotten longer now) that he brushes out of his eyes.

Eyeliner thick and sharper than a dagger, overblushed (just makes his skin look even paler) and a pouty mouth he chews on while he looks around.

She's not the only one who notices—across the quad, a group of basketball players coming out of the gym start a racket. –Oooweee! Hey Bryce, check this out! Here kitty-kitty-catboy, who you all dressed up for? Come on over, me and Brycey'll scrape some of that makeup off of you, make you look fucking DECENT again.

–Trent, hold up. I gotta stop a hate crime. –She starts to rap on the rear window. Old Ash would've frozen until the pack of boys consumed him; new Ash considers there might be worse things in the world than being beat to death by a group of cute jocks—

He notices Eu in the back of the car and turns quickly.

Comes towards them.

Trent glares and broods.

–THAT'S your friend?

–Uhm yes? Is there a problem?

–You didn't tell me he was some... pretty boy.

–I also didn't tell you he was Jewish. I also didn't tell you he was gay. I also didn't tell you he has a sister. I also didn't...

–He's gay?

–For fucks sake, Trent. LOOK at him.

Ash reaches the car and they both shut their mouths.

–Hi, thanks for waiting.

He smiles, and she can see Trent staring at him, struck, while he offers his hand through the rolled down window. Ash doesn't take it.

–I'm Ash.

–Trent. This is Nor. Norbert. ...You're sitting in the back with Eulalie?

He says it with a ring of alarm in his voice.

–Well, Nor's the navigator, right? He has to sit in the front. –Eulalie cuts in. Trent nods miserably, and Nor gets out; lets Ash folds himself up in the back, next to Eu. The engine roars and Trent puts on some music, before they get on the main drag. Eu takes out a little notebook and a pen, and she scribbles:

–Damn, boy. You trying to give us a heart attack?
–And passes it to him.

–Sorry, was I that late? –He scrawls. –I remembered last sec something else I had to quickly do...

–No! –She underlines the "no" three times. –I meant, you look HOT.

Ash trembles—he wants to return the compliment, but then Trent glares at him in the rear-view mirror. Eu puts her notebook away. The backseat is cramped and as both her and Ash are quite tall, they have no choice but to stretch out their legs against each other.

24.

It takes until dark to get to Vancouver and once they arrive, they murder many minutes in the dreary down-town, waiting for it to get darker—Nor says he's broke and doesn't want to eat in a sit-down restaurant. Ash seconds that—so they end up at a Plaid Panty; three painted up boys and one demonic girl, buying armfuls of Ho-Ho's and a half gallon of ToffeeNut coffee augment-ed with spritzes of Simple Syrup. Eu tries to sugar-talk the jaded cashier into letting her buy a pack of cigarettes for an after-dinner puff, but he won't budge—No ID No Sale; they take their booty outside, and are walking back to their car when three kids in a pickup tear out of the parking slot in front of them.

One of them screams out of his window, and Eulalie throws half a Ho-Ho at their car, while Nor dips Trent in a dramatic Hollywood kiss. Ash stares down at his boots;

the entire parking lot gawks at them and he wants to get back in their car, but Eulalie's not ready to go back: she starts twirling around in a Hostess-induced craze, her flouncy dovey skirt blows up—Ash can't stop staring at her thighs—she wears garters (he's never seen a real person wear garters), and fancy ruffled underpants and looks like the lovechild of Amy Winehouse and Marilyn Monroe from Hell. Trent catches his look on her; he puts his arm around Eu and they kiss—Ash shrugs and turns away. Back in the car—find the first place—which will then give them the address of the second place.

–Yeah, this party is top secret. –Eu confides to him in the back seat, and Ash elbows her in the side.

–You know, you got something on your face.

It's true, a smudge of white from one of the cream cakes—next to her shiny flamingo mouth, it's practically pornographic.

–That is what you think it is,–she purrs.

He rolls his eyes and wipes the cream off with a finger—Eu has the urge to lick it off him, but he surreptitiously smears it under the seat of the Mustang.

–We're here, kids, –Trent announces with a flourish. Ash looks out the window.

They've arrived at a cinder–block of gray industrial nothing.

25.

Outside, gray industrial nothing.

Ash's eyes strain when they step into the building—he's never been at a venue this big before. It's already packed with people dancing, every kind of beautiful, glittering person he could imagine—halfboys, catgirls, undefined people; the music is deafening trance—quicksilver, pheromones, push all through his body. Nor and Trent go ahead to settle bracelets with the ticket guy and Eu and Ash just stand by the door, watching the seething mass of dancers. Already, people are checking them out. Eu turns to him.

–So, we're clear on the rules, right? No drugs from anybody. And only drink water you opened yourself.

She gives him a small bottle she bought back at the convenience store. He asks:

–How are we getting back?

–The same way we came. This party goes all night though. I mean, all night. We're leaving at seven a.m. If I can't find you then because you're sucking face out back with someone, you're stuck here in the middle of butt–fuck Egypt, 'cause... I don't think Trent likes you too much. So he's not going to stick around to wait for you. Capish?

–Capish.

Eu talks tough, but he knows she wouldn't leave him. He wants to go dance with her, but Trent is already coming back. He passes out bracelets and then all four of them wander out onto the floor.

Or rather, they are absorbed by the floor, because

there are too many people to simply walk or dance wher-
ever. The crowd is an electric sea they offer their bodies
to.

And it accepts them.

26.

He never wondered where the term "trance" came from,
but now he thinks he may understand. A single word or
phrase is strained through the music—the beat pushes
against your ear-drum, over and over, subtle, the same,
until you slowly lose your mind. Ash started out dancing with Nor and Trent and Eu, but they've drifted from
each other. He would have loved to dance with Eulalie,
just the two of them, the way they used to, but Trent
hung off her the entire time, so openly possessive and he
couldn't get near her. She looked at Ash apologetically,
but didn't try to stop it. At one point, a boy came for Nor,
and he was led away. Now Ash is dancing alone deep in
the crowd; his eyes closed; letting the music rip him up
and put him back together again. He's been dancing for
so long, he can't feel anything anymore, neither the joy of
being alone, nor the pain of being alone—he's had nothing to drink, nothing to eat, nothing to smoke, nothing
to take—his body is high on the euphoria of emptiness.

A boy comes up to him, he can't see him, but then
he puts his head on his chest in that silver darkness—by
now, few people are sober, but maybe this person is, Ash
can't tell. The foreign boy puts a finger on his mouth, just
feeling it, draws the tip of his finger over his lips again

and again while he dances with him. Everyone around them is putting their hands all over everyone else. It's half-sexual and half-curious, as if they were just discovering the feel of another human being for the first time. He doesn't kiss anyone, just dances; the boy keeps looking at him; both of them are shy. But they don't own each other; he floats away; Ash lets him. Nobody belongs to him and he doesn't belong to anyone; just whoever stops with him for a moment. The DJ is good; the music streams effortlessly together, like a river that never begins and never ends—he wonders if he'd drop from exhaustion before he could stop dancing and has no idea how much time has passed—hours? Days?

He's moulted his trenchcoat and button up shirt long ago, all that sticks to his gaunt torso now is a white ribbed tank top, soaked in sweat. His eyes close again, so many people exist on all sides of him that he need not support himself anymore, just laying around upright is enough, swimming in a vast sea of sound and flesh and then in that vast sea, he feels someone draw closer to him. The body is warm, even in that ocean of heat, someone wraps an arm around him from behind, draws a finger gently down his throat; he feels their breath against him, but the person doesn't kiss him; and his blood dilutes; he wants them to—his eyes open—then he sees the person's arm, draped in front of him, the nails, ending in French-tipped neon. He knows this hand. He's drawn this hand—he knows the sinews of it, the bones of it. The flesh of how it works, connects, and how it moves.

He turns around, his eyes are closed, he doesn't have to look and she dances with him. He doesn't ask her any questions, just puts his head against her neck; she's taller than him, softer than him, they move, no kissing, just moving, slowly, he wonders if this is what it would be like, sex with a girl, it's like sex, he imagines, better, like when you want nothing to ever come between you. He presses into her; he's painfully hard, and it doesn't embarrass him, it doesn't embarrass her; he wants her then, his whole body does, he wants so much for her to kiss him, but she doesn't and he doesn't have the courage—they are so close, but his hold weakens; he can't stop it.

What is given is taken away.
The crowd brought her to him.
The crowd takes her away.

27.

–Trent's gone.

After a prolonged absence, Ash has finally found Eu again. She's by the door, talking to the bracelet guy, and she turns to him. It's 5 a.m. The music pumps as if it would never stop.

–What? –He stares at her. –What do you mean?

–Just that: Trent's gone. That dickwaffle up and left us here.

–But... why?

–While you were dancing your little heart out, Trentipoo and I had a lover's tiff.

–I don't like this thing between you two.

–There IS no thing. We're friends.

–Eulalie, do you think I'm stupid? He's been staring at you and hanging off you all night? You said he was gay.

–What the hell are you TALKING about? We danced together—one song!

–He thought you were too touchy with me, or me with you, whatever, and wanted us to leave early without telling you and strand you here. I told him I wouldn't do that, so then he got in a huff and left. Both of us.

–Oh man. I'm sorry, Eu. I didn't mean to cause trouble between you two.

–I mean, check out my face. Does it look like I give a shit?

–And the other guy? Is he gone too?

–Norbert? Oh, he's in another world. I think he's getting an 'oil-change' in the boy's bathroom.

–Delicate as always, Eu.

–You know me, baby. –She winks at him. –So, the million dollar question is, how the freak are we going to get home?

Ash looks over at the moiling day–glo crowd.

–We could try to make some new friends. With cars.

–And I know just the guy.

Eu pulls him into a corner.

–Hang on. –She takes out the tube of liquid eyeliner from her tiny leopard-print purse and tells him to close his eyes. Touches up his eyeliner, and brushes gloss on his lips. Glitters his collarbones and wipes his forehead with a tissue.

–…How do I look? –He bites his lip nervously and she ruffles his hair.

–Like a gorgeous under-fed down-trodden sec-
ond-world child *prostitute*. –She pushes him playfully.
–Now go get us a ride.
–And what about you?
–My feet ACHE. I'm taking a break.

28.

Ash trades a ride home for fifteen minutes of heavy
necking with a cadaverous-faced kid who says he's leaving soon. He wants to hold hands while they walk to his
rusting truck and Ash just manages to sink his into his
pockets and avoid calamity. Once they're in the cab, he
sits in the middle straddling the stick; Eu giggles next to
him and the driver apologizes for his reach every time
he reaches between Ash's legs to shift the car. Tom Jones
blares while they bump along—
what's new pussycat whoaaaaoaoaoaaaooooooo
They ask him to drop them off at the 7/11 on the
corner of the main boulevard by Ash's apartment. In the
parking lot, the guy stamps a final wet kiss onto Ash's
cheek and begs for his phone number, but he only smiles
enigmatically. Once they're in the safety of the over-lit
convenience store, Eu screeches with laughter.
–I can't believe you committed gender-fraud with a
diseased raver to get us home. Respect.
–I did not! I never lied to him...
–Then why was he calling you 'Ashley'?
–How should I know? I was trying to tune the whole
thing out. Anyway, he must have known. I mean, my
voice? And he was touching me... all over!

–He probably just assumed he'd hit the jackpot. A pretty girl with a sultry voice and a nice—

–You so owe me!

He's scrubbing slobby kisses from his face with a tissue while they cruise the snack aisle. The cashier and two trucker customers of an early suburban Saturday morning stare at the two rippling apparitions with distrust and fear. Eu makes herself a 16 ounce ToffeeNut–Mocha Vanilla Pumpkin Crème Blast at the hot drink dispenser and grabs two packs of Pop-Tarts (Brown-Sugar/Cinnamon); Ash buys orange mint gum. She's munching, he's chewing while they walk up the street to his apartment, tired and giddy. They're almost by his complex when a cop car pulls up to them; the officer swaggers out and shines a flash light in their eyes, trying to find signs of inebriation or drugs. There are none. They are both underage though, with no ID, and Eu has to convince the cop in her most dulcet tones that they really do live in the apartments just up the block and are on their way home. They were just on a little walk.

–Dressed like this? –The officer shines the light over them one more time. It's obvious he's bored and itching to detain them further, but finally lets them go.

–Fucking pigs. –Eu spits as the car drives away. –Don't they have anything better to do? So anyway, this is awkward, but I had... been expecting to spend the night at Trent's after the party. His parents are supposed to be out of town for some family reunion stuff he wasn't interested in going to and...

–And? –Ash stares at her naively and Eu's eyes wave heavenward. She makes the ok sign with her left hand

and starts to move the index finger of her right hand towards the O. Ash claps his hand to his head.

–Oh god, now I feel even worse for getting in your way.

Eu makes a face.

–Pu–leeeze. I've been pretending for way too long that Trent isn't an insufferable turd. But I lied to my mom about where I was going afterwards, and I didn't take my key. I guess I can just walk home now. My mom will be pissed if I wake her up this early, but I'll make something up...

–You could just come over. I was expecting you to anyway.

–You sure it's okay?

–Of course.

She walks into his apartment tiptoeing like she always does when they come home after a party—she is prone to forget that he doesn't have to sneak around his parents. Eu notes that the living room has started a treacherous backslide into its former state, though Ash claims that they've gotten inspired and have tried to not let it get too bad. She looks in the kitchen—it really is tidy in there, and she can detect only a faint shadow of the stench that used to hang in the air upon entering.

They walk up the stairs and fall into his room. After any party, club, or rave, their bodies are steeped in sweat and smoke and the saliva of strangers. They both need a shower. Ash showers first; Eu looks at his sketchbooks while he's gone, but he's quick. He gives her a clean towel and a T-shirt and boxers, and she showers slow.

Water runs all over her body, releasing the ache

from her bindered torso and high-heeled boots. His apartment may be crap, but the water pressure in his shower, she decides, is divine.

29.

When Eu comes back into his room, Ash is sitting in a tank top and sweat pants. He hasn't succeeded in completely removing all the eyeliner or glitter. Mid-sketch, he looks up.

   –I thought you fell in.

   –Your shower is just so nice, I couldn't resist. We have the shittiest pressure at my house.

   –Yeah, I know what you mean. This place absolutely sucks, but I wouldn't trade our shower for anything.

   She realizes then that she hasn't been in his room in over two months. Nothing much has changed though.

   –What's that you're doing? It looks kinda fun. –Eu teases gently and he smiles.

   –Being in the Orestaia was cool, but I'm really glad it's over. I NEVER had time to draw and it was starting to really get to me.

   She sits down on the couch. He silently hands her the Styrofoam cup from his desk and she sips coffee, stretches her legs. Ash draws casually, she sits in boxers, it's just after daybreak. They have the whole morning to themselves—his parents will be home soon, and immediately go to bed. His sister won't be home until early afternoon. Eu feels drained and utterly relaxed. At peace. They're tired, but neither of them makes a motion to sleep.

–Hey.

–Yeah? –She looks over, and he asks:

–Can I draw you?

Eu screws up her face.

–No! I don't have any makeup on. I've been up all night. I look like shit.

–What are you talking about? You look good. I've been wanting to draw you again for a long time.

–You have?

–Sure. –He drops his next sentence as if it were the most commonplace thing to say. –You really do have the perfect body, you know.

Eu almost spills her coffee. She wonders what's gotten into him, because while she knows she could be attractive, in certain lights, in certain things, that attraction was always removed from her physical raw self. To do with her personality; the things she puts on her body; the illusions she makes with makeup, clothes, accessories.

You have the perfect look? A plausible compliment.

But the perfect body?

Eu grimaces. –I totally gained weight this last month and my acne is worse than ever. Nice try, but flattery gets you nothing.

–I'm not trying to flatter you, I just want to draw you.

Her painted hand waves disdainfully.

–Oh gosh, my geesh, but if you want to draw me in these ratty old boxers and a T-shirt, be my guest.

Ash turns a color that can only be described as beet. He stares out the window.

–I was wondering. You know, I'm only asking because you draw too, so you won't misunderstand, well, if I could draw you... without them. I just once want to see what you really look like and put it on paper. I think it would be beautiful.

It's too much. Eulalie spits a mouthful of coffee on herself. She goggles at him.

–Ash... are you high?

–I'm sober! I'm totally sober and I'm serious. Look, it's not sexual, ok? But today especially I saw you, the way you looked, when we were dancing, remember that? We didn't talk, but I saw your hand on me, and I wanted to draw you so much, I was thinking about that then, but if you don't want me to, I totally understand and...

–Alright already.

Eu puts her coffee down, takes off her shirt without another word.

Slips off her boxers.

Lays her body out on the couch and she closes her eyes.

–Just do it.

He bites his lip and starts to draw.

Eu keeps her eyes closed.

Behind her eyes, thoughts hurricane around.

She thinks about her mom.

Her dad.

She thinks about her first girlfriend.

About Trent. And Micah.

She thinks about that feeling she got sometimes, like she was waiting for something.

Not a thing. Not what.

But who.

No, that's not true.

–You can move your head now, if you want to. I'm done with that part. Keep the rest of you still though, if you can.

–Sure thing.

Eu turns her head, careful to not also turn her body. She opens her eyes. Ash sits five feet from her, she sees him sideways. He leans over his art board, she hears him drawing. The graphite drives onto the paper. Occasionally Ash stops, he erases and rubs, the tips of his long fingers are blackened with the soot of graphite, skrrt skrrrt skrrt, but he doesn't speak and neither does she. They haven't turned on any music either, and the quiet electric hum and scratching sounds makes the inside of Eu's head all the louder.

Trent has been begging to see you naked for months and you always stave him off. Ash DITCHES you for months, but the second he asks—you jump.

Shut up. There was no JUMPING. HE begged ME to tag along tonight. HE insisted on drawing me. I love his art, and I'm letting him make me into more art. That's all. Also, he has a girlfriend.

You know that's all fake.

I've seen him kiss her. It is *not fake*. Finally got his little sis lookalike he was aching for. Honestly, he's so gross. I'm embarrassed I was obsessed with him for so long.

ObsesseD? Honest question, why the past tense?

Can you cut the smug tone and just fuck OFF?

–Eu did you say something?

–No, sorry. I'm just... nothing.

Ash watches moods flit across her face, he scribbles, puts his pencil down, studies his drawing. Picks his pencil up.

Chews the end of it, then looks down at the paper again.

Eu rotates her eyeballs so he's out of her line of sight, she figures, it's better if she doesn't watch him. Why make this all a big deal? She's been to figure drawing class before, not a chance she got often, but she's done it—observing the model with the detached eye of a sculptor molding a piece of clay. A breast is no longer a breast—it's a circle. A back becomes a plane, genitals a shadow. The body becomes a question to be solved, mysterious not because of its sex, but beyond it, perhaps just going back to the origins of the body, because there is no need for nudity to be sexual. She knows herself that it inherently is not.

Her eyes are closed, gently, she hears him scribbling, shading, erasing, touching, he rubs a shadow into place with his fingertip. He's looking at her—I'm the only thing that exists for him right now, she thinks, he's looking at me, trying to figure me out, where parts of me attach, at what degree and what angle. What of me is shadow and what is light. She remembers when they talked about drawing portraits. Months ago. I couldn't draw most people, he had said to her. Because it was too personal, too intimate, too passing their body through your body and interpreting it—fuck me like you draw a picture—*now we're getting to it, hmm? You know this is the closest you will ever come to him wanting to.*

She moves suddenly—Ash looks up.

–Hey, you broke the pose! I was at a good spot!

He groans and she grabs her shirt.

–I'm sorry.

–Eu, what's wrong? Are you cold? I can turn on the space heater...

She's shaking from head to foot.

–Shit, I'm sorry, I ruined your picture, but I can't anymore.

Hastily now, Eu covers herself, ashamed all of the sudden in her awareness. Her face turns to the wall, locked, and he stands up and puts the board down.

–Eu, I'm sorry, I didn't mean to be weird, I didn't mean to make you feel weird, but I really meant what I said, that I...

A sharp gesture from her makes him stop talking.

–It's fine. It's not your fault, I just got freaked out. It's been a long night. Can we please go to bed? I'm exhausted.

She knows the mood is ruined.

Ash nods, carefully puts the art-board away, orders his pencils. He sets the alarm to one p.m. Turns off the light. He slips into bed next to her.

They don't even say goodnight.

30.

That morning, Ash has a sex dream.

He does not have them often, but this one is vivid: He is with someone, he does not know who; it seems to be a woman, but he is not sure. They have a lithe, muscular body and are wearing something that appears to be a full-body latex suit. With a hole. They're in a place he can't recognize; the person is incredibly seductive, he wants them. In the dream, they make him beg for it. He rips more holes in the suit, peels it off of them, presses all over them, licks their entire body until they're wet everywhere, but it's still them who makes him beg for it.

He begs until the person lets him.

They fuck for hours and hours.

31.

He wakes up, warm—and mortified.

Because he knows without having to look that Eu is in bed with him, that she's asleep, and that he came; from the dream. God are you kidding me, this hasn't happened in SO LONG did it have to happen tonight of all nights? The sheets are steamed and wet, he would faint from shame if she woke up now. He doesn't know what to do, and is plotting a way to quietly change the covers without waking her, when he realizes that Eu isn't asleep. In fact, her eyes are open, on the ceiling, but she doesn't register him. Occasionally, her lids flutter and she softly moans. Covers up to her shoulders, but he can see her neck, glistening, bathed in sweat. He can't tell if she's feeling sick or sad or good. She looks all three.

–Eu?

A muffled noise, then she looks at him.

–What?

–Is something wrong?

Eu shifts her weight. Breathes out.

–Nothing's wrong.

–Ok. You just look. In pain. Or something.

–I'm fine. I'm just trying to come, –she tells him. Ash is certain he misheard.

–You're trying to... I'm sorry?

–I said, I'm trying to come.

–Like... *coming*, coming?

That's when he notices the slight movement under the covers. A flicker of light crosses her face and she bites her lip.

–You got it. I'm sorry I'm doing it in your bed, I should be more considerate and move to the bathroom, but I can't jerk off standing up. I never could. I have to be lying down in a bed. I'll wash the sheets when I'm done, and I'm sorry to be grossing you out...

He's nonplussed and almost speechless.

–No... not... grossed out... I just... Why?

She gasps, and then looks at him again.

–Oh my god, Ash, do you need a *power-point presentation* to get it? Because I'm fucking hot, ok? I was hot all night at the party, and the way you and I were dancing, yeah... didn't need that in my life just now, but you saw what happened to Trent though it probably would've sucked with him anyway, and then you did that naked drawing thing and right when I thought I might still make it until I got back to my own house and my own bed, you started having some fucking *sex dream* or something, and started moaning and rubbing up on me! In your sleep. That's when I couldn't take it anymore. So yeah... I need to come, and I'm going to come in your bed, and that's just the way it is. You were still sleeping when I started, so I thought you'd just sleep through it, but no such luck. I'll clean up when I'm done—just go back to sleep or go to the bathroom for ten minutes, if I'm weirding you out.

He looks at her, incredulous. Her face looks flushed, quite a bit so, and he wonders if she's close.

–Need any help? –He whispers then and she shakes her head viciously.

–Oh no, you don't. You are not going to screw with my head anymore. –She doesn't speak for three seconds, only sucks her lower–lip, and he watches her, fascinated. –You only want me because you just had a sex dream and maybe you're hot too, and now all of the sudden, I'm convenient for you. But you know what, I'm sick of you. –She sighs. –I'm sick of you, Ash.

–You know, it's really hard to have a conversation with you while you're touching yourself.

–Then stop talking to me and leave the room. I'm not doing this for you. I'm not trying to tease you into having sex with me. I honestly just want to get off, quickly and painlessly. I've given up.

–Given up what?

She stops, scrabbles to a sitting position, pulling the covers up over her.

–You know! You know, fuck it, I was actually starting to feel good about myself again, since we got sepa-
rated by the Orestaia, and then one night back with you
and I'm all messed up. Again. You'll touch me when I'm
dancing; you'll touch anyone when we're in a fucking
club—you'll kiss anyone; have your first time in a filthy
bathroom; get fucked by some slimy guy, but when we're
here, you know, in a nice, quiet place, where it could be
so good, with a person who cares for you, then I'm like...
disgusting to you. Even hugging me makes you flinch.
   –Eu... that's not...
   –I don't want to hear it. Let me concentrate.
   She starts to lay back down and he murmurs:
   –I just... I didn't know...
   She sucks in her breath. Laughing. Crying.
   –Oh my GOD, just shut UP. You KNEW. You AL-
WAYS knew, but you didn't care, because I'm not some
hot creep who wants to use you or a pretty girl with big
boobs you can show off at school.
   And you know? I used to think there was some
deep, complicated, or *artistic* reason for why you have
the power to make me feel so shitty about myself, but it's
all really simple. I'm big and loud and pockmarked, and
you're just a superficial *asshole*. It doesn't matter how
good we are together, I'll never be trophy enough for
you. Meanwhile, I'm no better than those pathetic guys,
whining about how you don't Give Me a Chance. So yes,
I hate you, and I fucking hate myself, and I really want
you to leave me alone.
   He can't though. He watches her, moves his hand
under the covers—

Her body feels like a wound to him, like some kind of livid sore. She feels one of his fingers brush her hand; it's light. Her eyes close, just for one moment, she lets herself, for one moment:

oh yes, oh yes, oh ash, please please please please, oh ash I've wanted you for s o f u c k I n g l o n g put your hands on me, your mouth, all over, please please please please ash please ash please ash do it ash do it ash do it do it do it DO IT.

No.

–Quote. We are not going to fuck. Ever. Un-quote.
He cringes.
–Eu, I don't want to …fuck you, ok? –He can barely say the word. –I just thought that I could…
–…That you could WHAT? Dude, am I speaking a foreign language?! I told you already I don't fucking want you, so what more the fuck do you WANT?
–Nothing.
He leans forward, to crawl over her and leave the room and leave her alone, and she's crying, not loud, but the tears come down hard, wetting her face, it reminds him of rain, of all the times they've walked outside and her face was made wet with rain, or snow. Wet with the seasons. He leans forward, her eyes close, his eyes close, should he, should he not, he doesn't know, but he kisses her then, like they kissed that one day on stage so long ago.
Like that one and only kiss she ever had from him, locked and kept safe inside. Kept safe from everything that had happened, all this time.

Sink, sink, sink, sink, sink.

Eu sinks deep underwater, her weight falling like a star.

Her body says to her, Say what you want I have the final word.

She lies in the pond of her own body.

This hasn't happened in so long, did it have to be tonight of all nights?

She wants to run away or at least apologize, but she's so exhausted.

Her skin tremors and shakes and she can't move her mouth.

At least now it will all be over.

He will be disgusted and it will all be over.

He will run away and it will be over.

Ash doesn't move.

His lips are parted, but no sound comes out.

She thinks dully. I have to get up.

I have to try.

He's still leaning over her, silently, staring. His right hand on her wet stomach, over her wet shirt.

Eu shivers every time his hands move.

He looks like he wants to ask her a question.

Finally, she can speak—

–Oh god, dude, I'm so so sorry.

–What for? It's okay.

–No. It's NOT. NONE OF THIS has been okay. I'll change your sheets.

–I'll do it tomorrow. You must be so tired. Do you want to sleep?

Eu doesn't answer. She's scared she's going to start crying again.

And he's still petting her stomach.

He kisses her on the cheek, the forehead, and Eu figures, what difference does it make anymore.

He kisses her on the mouth and she feels them both hurtling toward the same direction.

–Is this okay? He asks and she turns her face.

–Ask YOURSELF. You said never. Not me.

–Devotchka, –he says in another language. –I want to.

–I don't know what you just said.

–I said, that I want to...

Shudder, shudder.

He's waiting for an answer.

–Did you say something? Ash murmurs.

Eu says:

-I said, beg me.

He begs her.

He begs her.

And she says nothing, but does finally nod.

And Ash looks like he is genuinely happy.

He tells her, he's never been with a girl before and he doesn't want to disappoint her.

She tells him, she's never been with anyone before. And maybe she'll disappoint him first.

The first time is short. Ash can't help it.
It feels *weirder* than she thought it would.
But then there is the next time. And the next.

They pass out just as he slaps the alarm silent.
Their bodies are numb and sated and sore.
They hold each other in the hot wet, asleep.
Like two embryos in one womb.

33.

Lena opens the door to their bedroom door at 2:38 p.m. that next Saturday afternoon and stops dead at the door.

Her brother is lying in his bed, naked, intertwined with that big black–haired girl who used to come here all the time before. Both are gone to the world.

Lena stares at her brother.

She knows she should close the door and give them their privacy, but she can't look away.

Ash doesn't do that. He's not like that.

She watches them sleeping and her heart hurts for things she knows she cannot hurt for. The pain is quiet, dark, deep.

Why this person, Ash? Everything about her. It's so loud and aggressive and... UGLY.

The girl shifts in bed and Lena freezes, but the other's eyes stay closed. She doesn't wake up. Her brother, still asleep, pulls closer to her. Lena watches him put his face to her neck. In his sleep, he smiles.

I guess ...he is happy with her, she thinks then, and finally closes the door.

She never tells him or anybody that she saw.

34

On the following Monday morning, Ash opens his locker in school and a folded note flutters out from the bottom. He picks it up. Unfolds it. Reads it.

It's typed. 12 point. Times New Roman. Addressed to no one.

Ash stares at the note. It's the perfect end to a perfectly surreal weekend. He puts it in his sketchbook, unsure of what to make of it. It could be an anonymous joke; it could be a mistake; it could be Eu; then he feels someone slip a hand into his back pocket. He turns abruptly, his heart races. Calms.

–Oh. It's you.

Fiona presses her face to his.

–Were you expecting someone else? I couldn't reach you all weekend, I was so worried! Where were you?

–At home, doing homework, –he mumbles, avoiding her eyes. –I had two papers due today.

He's still holding his sketchbook, and starts to slip it into his bookbag. She perks up.

–Oh, is that your book of drawings?

–Sure.

–You've still never let me see. Are you ever going to show me?

His tone is rough.

–I told you. I don't show people.

–Well, you could draw me and then show me just that.

–I said that too. I don't just... draw anyone.

–Hey! I'm not 'anyone', jeez.

–That's not what I meant and you know what I meant.

Fee takes a step back from him.

Her big wide eyes fill with tears.

–What is wrong with you today? You're so grumpy with me this morning when I didn't even get to talk to you at all weekend.

Ash is washed with guilt.

–I'm sorry. Really. It's not your fault, I'm just really tired.

She falls into step with him and he thinks that the one person he can safely eliminate as the author of the note is his own girlfriend. They walk to their first period, which they happen to share: English Literature.

Now that he's apologized and attempts to act interested, Fee talks animatedly about the injustice of the drama club's latest call-back list.

Ash listens, nodding considerately at all the appropriate intervals. He's never been so happy to walk to class, knowing that when the bell rings, she will HAVE to stop talking to him.

Across the hall, he sees Eu walking alone, her brutal gait cuts a path through the wave of kids, her buckles and chains all jangle, and she's listening to something on her headphones. He can tell it's heavy by the way her black eyes flash: hardcore, or metal, and she's so absorbed that she doesn't see him, doesn't see anyone. They're almost right next to each other when she looks up, and their eyes connect. Her blackpolished lips mouth the words:

He knows they can't talk now, doesn't expect her to try, but he wants her to give him a sign. A smile. A nod.

A blink, anything that says. Yes, I wrote that note. Yes, Friday happened.

He's openly looking at her even with Fee next to him, but she pointedly avoids eye contact. Keeps walking. Chill air rushes to fill the space behind her.

–Right Ash? I mean, how could he do that? –Fee nudges him and he has no idea who he's denouncing.

–Yeah. What an asshole.

His mind is a million miles away.

35.

Now Ash deliberates for three days.

During this time, he is utterly distracted. That afternoon, he goes home and spends the rest of his hours lying on his couch, turned to the wall, listening to music. At first, Lena decides to let him be, but finally, she feels like she has to talk to him. She has to say something. She kneels on the ground behind him and taps him on the shoulder. Ash pulls off his headphones, but doesn't turn around.

–Do you need something?

–No... Ash... what's wrong?

–I don't know. ...Maybe nothing.

At school he draws furiously, the urge to draw is so strong, his hand itches for it. He keeps a ruled sheet of notebook paper close by, so that he can quickly pull it over his open sketchbook at a moment's notice, should a teacher or student pass by and most of the times, it works just fine. Only in third period pre-calculus does he slip. He'd taken his sketchbook out and has his sheet of paper to cover, but as Mr. Langweilig goes on, he becomes lost in drawing. He draws her as he has been drawing her for the last 48 hours; from his memory—the memory of their last Friday and of every day before that. He draws her standing, sitting, lying down, her face close up, angry, teeth glinting in a smile, crying, he draws her in her sharp black clothes, as long and formless as she could make herself, binding her chest; he draws her naked, he draws her leaning over him, sweating, the way he remembers her big hands braced against his collarbones. He draws her well-lined black eyes, her strong eyebrows, her long straight nose with the hump, the pitted scars on her face. He sketches and shades and outlines her, with breasts, with a flat masculine chest, with less body fat, with more body fat, with a shaved head, with long hair, and for a while, he deceives himself and says it isn't her, that he is drawing an anonymous androgynous figure, an alien, a demon, an angel, like many of the other figures he'd drawn in the past, but of course he knows it's not true. He draws and draws and draws and the third time his teacher says his name, so loud, the entire class cowers (ASHER!!!) he looks up, wide–eyed and openly surprised.

–Mr. Langweilig.

–Yes, Mr. Machnik. Thank you for finally joining us on planet Earth. I was asking you what this value here is. –He raps his pencil against a tick on a graph on the overhead projector.

–I'm sorry, I wasn't paying attention.

That he admits it so readily seems to profoundly enrage his teacher. Langweilig descends from his desk like a sweltering rain cloud.

–Give me that book, –he booms. –We're all going to have a look at what has you SO occupied.

Before his teacher can reach his desk, Ash slams his sketchbook closed and places it against his chest, arms over it.

–No.

His teacher seems surprised at his resolve, and disappointed that this will not culminate in a public humiliation spectacle.

–Very well. I've told you before, that this is not an art class, and while I'm sure that drawing p o r n o g r a p h y. –He stretches the word out and the class collectively snickers.

–It's not... pornographic! –Ash says hotly.

–...That drawing pornography is infinitely more interesting than the Lower Bound Theorem, I personally find your lack of attention in my class extremely disrespectful. Pack up your things, and get yourself down to Principal Recht's office. We will continue this *aesthetic debate* after class.

Ash drudges down to the principal's office. The secretary knows him by sight, still, she must admit, it's been months since she's last seen him.

–Missed us? –She jibes and Ash stands in front of her, with his book–bag, drooping.

–I'm supposed to see the principal.

–You've been doing so well lately! What on earth could you possibly be in trouble for this time? Setting things on fire again? Fist-fighting?

–I wish. Just spacing off in class.

–As usual! Take a seat, space cadet. She's in a meeting, but she should be back in ten minutes.

Ash nods, smiles at her, takes a seat—he always felt like the secretary was on his side. He waits until she's turned her face back to her computer screen, then takes out his sketchbook again. The urge to take it out and hold it is almost magnetic, but he doesn't look at the drawings now. He looks at the very front flap, where he had pasted the note he'd found in his locker. Since then, he's read it a hundred times, until he had it memorized, still reading it over and over. Like a secret:

I've been yours since the day I first saw you, do you know it? I don't think, you're always caught in your own world. And that's ok, you like to think, I like to watch you thinking, try to scale your Wall, it tore me up, I tore myself up. Getting to the Top and had a nasty Fall—broke into pieces, Two, four, eight, sixteen, thirty two, all the way until the End, When night was day and black was white and I was bled, For You, I told myself I'd stop, I wouldn't love you—such a Lie.

You are so lovely, out and in, and now I'm Yours— until I die.

Each day, he is more certain that Eulalie wrote it. He *wants her* to have written it.

36

On the afternoon of the third day, he looks for Eulalie, because he knows he'll have to find her if he wants to talk. She won't come to him. He spots her out in front of the school. She's sitting on a bench, studying something next to her on the wood, when he moves over and sits down. He's too excited and nervous to pay attention to whatever she was inspecting.

–Hey, –he says. –I've been looking all over for you. You been in hiding?

He smiles at her. and she doesn't smile back.

–Well, I'm here now, malchik, so. ...ooh, are those your lucky suspenders? What's the occasion?

–Nothing, I just had an urge for them today. Just an urge.

–Can't fight the urge, I guess. I must say, I do admire your balls, coming to school in that get-up. How many people have tried to kill you today?

–Nobody. Yet. Anyway, Eu, I'm just going to jump in... About last Friday...

Her hand shoots out in a 'stop' motion and he shuts his mouth.

–Ash. Listen. About last Friday, I said a lot of crazy shit. We both did... a LOT of crazy shit. Can we just leave it at that? I'm still embarrassed about how I acted, and you don't have to worry.

–What do you mean?

–I mean, you don't have to worry! You think because of what happened, that I'm going to be weird now, or expect something from you. But I know how you feel about me and ...that's fine. I'm not in love with you.

His jaw clenches.

–...You're ...*not?* ...But what about... the note?

She raises an eyebrow and he doesn't care; he tears open his bag and drags out his sketchbook.

–Come on, do not tell me you didn't leave this in my locker! I found it on Monday, after—after—

He thrusts the sketchbook in front of her, opens it to the inner flap and Eu reads the note with interest. She gets to the last line and wrinkles her nose, and he stares down at his feet:

–You know, I thought it was really pretty. Nobody's ever written or done anything like that for me before.

Eu snorts.

–You thought it was really pretty, what? We're missing an adjective here, Ash. Really pretty gay? Really pretty sappy?

He tears his sketchbook out of her hands.

–What the fuck is wrong with you? I just said that I thought it was... beautiful and I appreciated it so much, so why can't you admit that you wrote it?

–Because I didn't!

–Then who did?

–How the hell should I know? But hey, here's a wild stab in the dark. Maybe it's that girl who's *licking your face* in the hallway every day. Why don't you ask her?

–Yeah fucking right. We both know that there's no way that she did.

–How would I know that? You've literally never told me a single thing about her. She could be a poet and I wouldn't know it—

–Ok, that's it... get up.

Without even thinking, his hand reaches out, grabs the lapel of her black coat, pulls her up towards him. He yanks so hard, she actually rises, rolls to her toes. Surprise flickers in her eyes.

–What's this, malchik? You want to fight me? You know that kicking your ass is just going to *turn me on*, right?

Someone from across the courtyard looks over. Ash lowers his voice. Shakes.

–Stop. I know you wrote this, I know it, because only you like me like... this... and that's how I like you too, so please. Eu. I am asking.

His heart is pounding so hard, he's certain she can hear it.

Maybe she can.

Eu closes her eyes. Opens them again. Like she's resetting herself.

Her expression is interesting.

She says:

–Hey, will you do me a favor?

–What?

–Close your eyes.

–Why?

–Are we playing Twenty Questions? Damn, boy. Just do it.

Ash studies her for a moment.

He decides to humor her.

The sun is weak—He closes his eyes.

He hears her breathing.

She hears his breathing.

Eu raises a hand. He feels it stop in front of his face.

His breath gets shallow—what is she doing? Her breath stops.

Her fingers find him—he gives a slight jerk at their touch.

So does she, but then they both relax—

His cheekbones—his brows—his eyelashes—his nose.

The light dent in his chin.

Up, over the slight dent in his lower lip.

The philtrum.

She traces it with the tip. Once. Twice. The air is in overdrive— it swells—

She sighs. It breaks.

Opening his eyes, he sees that hers are still closed and she's smiling.

–That... was the favor? –He breathes out. –You wanted to touch my face?

–No, –she says. –The favor is, that today I want to draw you. Can I?

–Sure. But do I have to be, –He reddens again. –naked?

–As you wish, milord. –She winks. –Seen it all anyway.

He pushes her. Spins her around. It's hard to though, he doesn't have the body strength, so she picks him up and spins him around instead. They start to walk; she tells him about this new band she wants to go see with him next weekend. If he's up for it.

Sodomy and Garfuckle. A punk tribute band.

–Seriously, you'll never think of "Kodachrome" the same... 'when I think back on all the chicks I fucked in high school der ner ner ner ner ner ner ner der ner ner ner ner ner ner ner'

He doesn't tell her that he broke up with his girlfriend that morning, not yet, and that he's gotten tickets for them both to go see the Paul Klee exhibition showing next month downtown.

And she doesn't tell him about her handywork on the bench, where he'd just been sitting.

Maybe that's just as well.

It's Eu's theory that walls can be painted over, but if you carve your love into wood, it can never die.

Still it has to be kept a secret. So she keeps what she carved into the bench a secret, even from him.

a + e 4ever

It's early early spring.
Soon trees are flowering.

Epilogue

By fall that next school year, nobody at McMillan High remembers Asher Machnik anymore.

To the Tall Kid, he dissolves into a memory of a person who sexually confused him.

To his girlfriend Fiona, he blends into the flash mob of boys she will date until she marries, and then, the cast of the "Orestaia" no longer exists.

They are now the cast of "A Streetcar Named Desire."

Ash's family moved away suddenly towards the end of the summer, when his parents got laid off. Neither he nor Eulalie were surprised. He had warned her—layoffs and debts kept them constantly in motion. His family's new plan was to go back down to California. Their last night out, those two danced so hard they all but collapsed—when the party ended, they walked the rest of the night together, deep into the morning; holding hands. Talking.

Eu gave him an expensive color pencil set as a goodbye gift; he gave her a big art book on Kandinsky and a cherry pie he baked for her. With his sister's help.

They drew a final portrait of each other—Eu had shaved her head completely not long before, and Ash's hair by then had grown back down to his jaw. They swapped studded bracelets. Made each other one last playlist.

Now it's the sixth week of her senior year.

Eulalie Mason sits in stall two of the southern hall's bathroom.

The walls are freshly repainted from summer.

Girls again have a pristine wall on which to scrawl the names of those they'd like to fuck.

The hot names of this year include Jacob Heiss and Ami Schone, but she's not interested in the new list.

Finding a chip in the paint (already!), she starts to lightly scratch at it with a glitter purple nail.

Only Eu remembers that Ash's name is under there.

About the author

Ryszard Merey is originally from Hungary and now lives in Germany with his family. He is a writer, illustrator, book designer, ex-mannequin and future kooky old man. His favorite shape is the hexagon.

About the press

tRaum Books is a tiny press dedicated to unconventional formats, with a focus on queer and trans narratives. You can visit us online at http://www.traumbooks.com